VOODOO CHILD

Midnight Sleeper

Book 3

ISBN: 0-9884911-2-5
Paperback ISBN 13: 9780988491199
Hardback ISBN: 978-0-9884911-20
eBook ISBN: 978-0-9884911-4-4

www.raederlomax.com

VOODOO *midnight* *Sleeper* CHILD

Book 3

RAEDER LOMAX

"If you want power for the sake of power, you'll always
live a life of tragedy, because to keep it you must be cruel."
Elke, Midnight Sleeper 3

For Genya, Leah, Lazar Wolfe, Herschel, Uncle Joe
Rosmarin: pilot in the Abraham Lincoln Brigade.

Late Winter 1926
Berlin

1

Hotel Esplanade

Addison Prevette
Prevette Hall Plantation
Clarksdale, Mississippi

Dear Old Foe,

I do hope everything is going well back home, because over here things are not. Once again, a faction of the Black Reichswehr nationalists has stolen the hotel mail and were caught with one of my letters. The Polizei returned it to me and told me that the girl connected to the first theft was an American and then for some dumb reason I was warned that meddling in German affairs was considered spying and that the penalty was death, and that I would be tied face down to a board in the prison yard so that the executioner could cleanly chop my head off with an axe that he carries around in a special black bag wherever he goes. I kindly reminded the police that they were mixing up girls. They didn't care. They wanted to know why someone my age was in Berlin without her parents and just how long did I plan on staying? And did I have any friends or family living here? Plus, a lot of other nosey questions that only a snake would ask. Inspector Degler, he's from the Berlin Political Office at police headquarters, Die Rote Burg, or the Red Castle, wanted to know why I spoke German so well. I told him because I've got brains. He told me that I'd be hearing from him soon enough. I told him that I had heard enough.

Now about what they call the Fatherland over here. I feel as if I'm in two worlds: one that can be touched and the other that is way out of touch. Not a day goes by that you aren't confronted with blind hobblers struggling along on bony crutches that easily snap or amputated men from the war who follow you with long eyes as they shake the Pfennigs in their cups while you hurry past their nightmares; and then there are the street walkers from inflation days who offer services so extensive that their skills are now demographically mapped for tourists. And if that weren't enough, the democratic government has no spine. It seems they made a deal with the Reichswehr (the legitimate German army) to crush the Reds—who are heavily financed by the Soviets—and in the bargain the Reichswehr has been allowed to function independently from the government, which allows them to support the paramilitary groups hell bent on insurrection, such as the Black Reichswehr who are nothing but a bunch of crybabies who lie through their teeth. If I've learned anything from them, it is that when someone is angry or feels betrayed—even if he has *never* been betrayed— he cares not whom he hurts nor what he says, but only that the result is painful.

This all became apparent aboard the SS Albert Ballin that we sailed on from New York to Hamburg. We met a former Prussian army Major who just happened to know Zola from her days in Berlin. His name is Magnus von Coors, and he is a real nuisance as well as the leader of the right-wing faction Die Deutsche Nationale Freiheitspartei, otherwise known as the DNF. I did not want to bother you about him in the last letter, but I will now. My feud with him started with his dislike of Beau. The Major flat-out asked me in German, as he speaks no English, if Beau was my nigger lover. I told him I'd go for Beau any old day over him and so he indulged in a long lecture on zoology, which he knows nothing of, as his system of beliefs emanates from anger and resentment, and not science. Having said that, Zola won't divulge anything about what went on between her and the Major after the war, but then you know how Zola is when she has something you want; she becomes a real snoot. So, for now, I've had to endure the Major's unctuous company and Zola's nose up in the air. By the way, she's at the door right now saying that she's hungry (her dinner bell is always ringing). Oh, and she says thank you for whatever you did for her, of which she won't tell me, but I trust that you will inform me in your next letter. And please tell Mama to stop worrying about me over here because it won't do her any good over *there*.

One more thing, tonight, we're going to see Valeska Gert perform the *Orgasm* in a cabaret near the Kurfürstendamm, probably sometime after midnight. She's a wicked girl, this Valeska, but then so is her charm. But first, on the Kurfürstendamm, we're going to see the sensation of Berlin and all of Europe: the Voodoo Child at the Himmel u. Hölle Kabarett (Heaven and Hell), and it seems no one can get enough of her. I shall tell you all about her in my next letter.

One other thing, please inform your son, who happens to be my brother, that I sent him that new 35mm Leica 1-A camera, the one you kindly paid for, to take pictures of Mama whenever she opens my mail, so that I can send her to jail for being a snoop.

Love and miss you,
Shelby
(Your least rebellious child.)

2

Große Stern Allee

A black Ford-Werke sedan drove out of Berlin's vast Tiergarten Park and made a sharp turn into Große Stern Allee, one of the many streets that radially fed out of the city's multiple crossroads. The sedan headed for Emil Hugenberg who was ambling down the road lost in thought over the consequences of the American Dawes plan that was now threatening to save Germany from economic ruin, as well as propping up the democratic Weimar Republic. The sedan pulled to a stop. At first, Emil Hugenberg couldn't identify the men behind the rain spotted windshield. One of them got out and told Emil Hugenberg to get in. They then drove off.

3

On Short Notice

Zola rushed out of the Hotel Esplanade with an umbrella that she couldn't open. She handed it to her cousin Shelby and said, "So what the Major's a little weird? The war made us all nuts."

Shelby said, "Well, I know a lotta weird people who weren't in any war, including Cousin Marston, but the Major, more than anyone else, has got this nasty habit of needling you with his damn self-importance."

"And you've got this nasty habit of needling him back."

"You get what you give," Shelby said, as she got the umbrella open. "I thought it wasn't supposed to rain tonight."

"Well, a lot of things aren't supposed to happen," Zola said, "and you don't have to marry the Major. He's just gonna be with us for tonight and might even pay for everything, and that's just fine by me."

"You're rich now," Shelby said. "You don't need him to pay for anything."

"Maybe, but he knows people here, and when the police left the hotel, he saved your butt."

"From stealing my own mail?"

"From sitting in jail," Zola said.

"Not from sitting with him tonight."

"Seems you forget that the police thought you were tied up with that American girl from the first mail theft and the Major set them straight."

Shelby said, "The Major doesn't do anything unless it's good for him."

Beau on his way out of the hotel came over and said to Shelby, "Concierge gave me this here note for you. Says it was marked important."

Zola said to Shelby, "You in more trouble?"

Shelby read the note and said, "…No. It's from my mother."

A bellboy, wearing a blue chin strapped brimless coffee can cap with a gold stripe around the top, handed Shelby another note. She read it and said, "…Seems Mrs. Remley had to visit someone on short notice—must be why she didn't answer her door before."

Beau said, "She say where she went?"

"No," Shelby said, "but she hopes to meet us later on tonight." A taxi drove up to the front entrance. Beau got in last with a long hard case in hand.

Zola said to him, "What're you bringing that for?

"I just got a call from the cabaret we goin' to," Beau said.

"I thought you sold that saxophone to some German cigarette maker on the boat over," Zola said.

"Well," Beau said, "he didn't wanna pay enough and I didn't want to sell it enough."

"Why're you bringing it to the cabaret?"

"You remember them colored boys on the boat over?"

"That jazz band?"

"Yeah," Beau said to Zola, "They gonna be playin' at the cabaret we goin' to and the fella on the saxophone, he off with some girl, so the boys asked iffen I could fill in for him."

Shelby put a cigarette to her lips and said, "…Does that mean you'll be leaving me?"

Beau struck a matchstick. Their eyes met in the hottest part of the flame. "Ain't easy leavin' you, miss……"

4

Grunewald, Berlin

The Hespelbrunn mansion, once a grand hunting lodge, faced the Grunewaldsee, a sleepy lake known for its short-toed treecreepers, mute swans, and Eurasian coots that patrolled its grassy shores. Sarah Revenlöw Remley's taxi entered the mansion's long winding driveway and parked under an orbed portico that gave shelter from the briny winter air. A footman came forth and opened the taxi door. He took Sarah into a vaulted hallway that was walled with heirloom portraits of horsemen in powdered perukes, mounted stag heads, coats of arms, and medieval weapons that once chopped off body parts after horses clashed. Guarding the library was a knight's armor in silver cuisses, greaves, and pauldrons shining. In each gauntlet was a cleaver falchion for making mincemeat of humans. The butler showed Sarah into the library and shut the door behind her.

All around her were vast shelves of books that covered the walls. Sumptuous leather armchairs crowded the center of the room. Side tables were set with silver matchstick dispensers and unfinished drinks. A burning cigarette left an ash that crept across an ashtray. A tin of Walküre Gold Tip Cigarettes with the figure of Brünnhilde in a winged helmet and flowing hair was on the large mahogany desk right off the great window that faced the Grunewaldsee. The desk was bare except for a telephone and a cloisonné lapel pin that glowed under a lamp. A secret door, flush to the wall, opened. A tall gray-haired man, in his seventh decade, emerged. He bowed and put his lips to the top of Sarah's hand and said, "Good evening, Frau Remley." He spoke to her in German as he did not know any English. "It is a great pleasure to meet the wife of Ellis Remley. A true patriot and supporter of our cause. A man who could not be swayed by the petty concerns of people who are more fright than fight."

Sarah withdrew her hand. "Where's my cousin Egon?"

"I have the pleasure, madam."

"Who are you?"

"An old friend of your husband's."

"What was his cause?"

"Had he not spoken of it?"

"No," Sarah said, "and where's my cousin?

"No need to worry. I got here as soon as I could."

"As soon as *you* could?"

"My associates and I."

"Associates…?"

"Friends of your husband."

"I suppose they have names," Sarah said.

"I fear that you may not know them."

"Are you a man who fears?"

"Not at all."

"Then who are they?"

"Friends," he said.

"Have you or they a name?"

"We are traditional radicals," he said.

"*Traditional* radicals…?"

"Decent, honest men, frustrated with democracy."

"You're sure it's not something else?"

"Not when it comes to the soul of Germany," he said.

"You speak of the soul as if politics and religion are one and the same."

"Should not the state have a soul that is nationally inspired?"

"The religious soul and the political soul are of two different notions," Sarah said.

"And that is the great calamity of the modern nation state."

"In fact," she said, "it is its great achievement to have separated the two and to do God's work based on judgement sourced from reason and not from hocus-pocus, despite the internal and external stimuli that invariably foul one's intentions."

"You speak as if you know God," he said.

"Enough to know that you misread his intentions."

"His intentions are within all of us, and so we are always acting on his behalf."

"That is *your* intention, not necessarily his," Sarah said.

"Then I fear that you suffer from the same political misgivings as do the Social Democrats."

"What misgivings are those?"

"Frau Remley, the German Volk isn't fooled. It knows that the Weimar government is cowardly trying to accrue even more power by supporting the American Dawes Plan."

"And what is cowardly with compassion? Your country desperately needs financial help."

"Not if it's driven by foreign interreference and cultural pollution aimed at weakening the blood of our people," he said.

"There is nothing in the Dawes plan that requires you to be anything than what you already are."

"Nonsense," he said. "America's silly notions of modernity and progressiveness are creeping into our society with its soup kitchen denial of Darwin and it confusion of equality as an equalizer of men. But I can assure you that those who have been genetically vetted by blood and history for positions of power are losing their patience."

"Then you've misread Darwin, and if you believe that other baloney then you are a dangerous man."

"Dangerous…?"

"Yes," Sarah said, "in that what you say is an interpretation bred by malfeasance and not genetics."

"Frau Remley, what's to come is historically inevitable."

"If not laughable."

"I don't see you laughing."

"When a person laughs to himself, he is never heard," Sarah said. "Why don't you try selling your precious blood and see how much you get for it?"

"Frau Remley, our precious blood is not for sale."

"But your silly ideas are—and just where in America have you tested your muddled theories?"

"Frau Remley, what I've seen from afar more than justifies not having been there. Now, what about the letter?"

"Letter…?"

"From Ellis, your husband, which was to have been sent. He said that if anything should ever happen to him that you would fulfil his duties."

"Is that why you're here?"

"It's why *you're* here, Frau Remley. Now, we need the letter."

"Sir, if you tell me nothing of the letter, then I can do nothing about it."

"Frau Remley, your husband said that you would bring it to us, if he couldn't."

"That *I* would bring it…?"

"He trusted you."

"Ellis never trusted me with anything other than our children and even then, he didn't."

"Time is of the essence, Frau Remley, and I need that letter. We are all waiting for it."

"Are you a member of one of those political combat leagues that I've been reading about?"

"Had Ellis spoken to you of this?"

"He never said a word to me, but what do I know, I cannot approve."

"With all due respect, Frau Remley, I care not what you approve."

"And you care not that you are rude to a woman."

"I am not rude at all," he said, "but then the fault of women is to mistake the plucking of a chicken with the affairs of state, which completely goes against their inborn sensitivity for children and animals that undermines their ability to make hard decisions. A mother loves her child even if he is a murderer, and that is a weakness men don't have."

"She may love him, yes, but not his crime."

"The heart speaks differently."

"Sometimes it speaks not at all."

"Then I will speak in its place," he said. "Those who wish to hand Germany over to subversive forces, including external enemies, will be sorry when we strike the fatal blow."

"You seem to have a lot of enemies. Have you no friends?"

"Frau Remley, our side has many friends. Now, please, hand over the letter."

"I have no letter, sir."

"…You did not bring it?"

"I didn't bring it anywhere," Sarah said.

"Then it's at the hotel."

"What is your name, sir? Or do you fear my knowing it?"

"Emil Hugenberg."

"…You mean the industrialist?"

"Yes," he said. "Now the letter, as I'm pressed for time."

"I have no letter," Sarah said.

"You were instructed to give it to me."

"No one instructed me of anything."

"Frau Remley, I do not know what your problem is, but it will only get worse if you continue to divert yourself at our expense. Now, I advise you to hand over that letter."

"I told you that I do not have it."

"Frau Remley, you did not come all the way to Germany, at this unique moment, just to see the Berlin Zoo."

"That's exactly why I came," she said.

"Then…" Emil Hugenberg said, stiffening up as if having been prodded, "it was a pleasure meeting you."

"I think not, or you wouldn't be leaving so soon."

"Frau Remley, you're not a woman to leave soon, but there is a car waiting for me. I will visit you tonight at your hotel to finish our business and get the letter."

"Without invitation?"

"My name is invitation enough," he said. "And you *will* have the letter."

"Or what…?"

"Frau Remley, life is short as is one's patience. Since you say that you don't have it now, I will respect that, but you will hand it over, to me, at your hotel, tonight."

"Otherwise…?"

"We'll have to get to know each other the old-fashioned way." With a slight bow, he disappeared through the paneled wall.

Sarah went over to her cousin Egon's big desk and dipped a pen into the inkwell and left a simple note: "Where the hell were you?" She then reached for the cloisonné lapel pin and ran her fingers over it as if to wipe away its intrigue. The library door opened. She closed her hand over the pin. The butler, in shadow, said, "Frau Remley, your car is waiting……"

5

The Glass Eye

The taxi turned east on Leipziger Straße and flew past the grand Wertheim emporium that was fortified by five round topped arches and a vast street side loggia protecting pedestrians from inclement weather, but nothing else. Shelby said to Zola, "You still haven't answered my question."

"I can't answer what I don't know."

"Look, I find it a little odd that you've got all these names. Everywhere we go someone calls you by a different one. Why is that?"

Zola, more interested in the double decker bus in front of them, yelled at their driver in German. "I said get us there fast. *Not* kill us." The driver, a war veteran, swerved around the bus. She said to Shelby, "He's gonna kill us."

"Answer my question."

Zola grabbed the armrest and said, "Where's Bob? I thought he was coming with us tonight."

Shelby said, "Mr. Benchley is first meeting up with Brayton Hills, that reporter from Chicago, to get the lowdown on the mail theft that he wants to write about in *The New Yorker*." She then gripped the edge of the rear seat as the taxi veered to the left and then to the right.

Zola, eyes glued to the bus in front of them, said, "Well, I've got a meeting with that editrix of *Die Dame* tomorrow for a story that they're doing on the Voodoo Child. I'll ask her if she can get us any more information about those people who robbed you."

"I got a better idea," Shelby said. "Why don't you ask her why you get called by a different name wherever we go?"

"I'm beautiful; that's why," Zola said, nose up in the air. Zola then grabbed onto Shelby as the taxi sharply veered left. "This damn cabbie shouldn't be allowed to drive with a glass eye in his head."

"How do you know it's glass?"

"I was a surgical nurse during the war, or have you already forgotten?"

"I haven't," Shelby said, "but how do you know it's glass?"

"Because we had boxes of them at the hospital and every time I opened one, hundreds of eyeballs stared straight at me and that's what's in his head."

"That still doesn't tell me why someone at the Kakadu Bar called you Hedwig last night," Shelby saying it the German way with the "v" sound. "And that guy with the silver cocaine box at the Birkenheide Cabaret called you Gertrude and you answered like you had known him all your life."

"I don't remember him at all," Zola said.

"How can you forget someone totally nude except for a top hat on his head?"

"That's the way they are in nudie cabarets," Zola said. "They're all loco. It has to do with the war."

"Well, if that's true," Shelby said, "how come you're the only nut that gets called by a different name wherever we go?"

The taxi driver flew past Spittel-Markt, another Berlin hub where the avenues dangerously crossed over."

"Look," Zola said, trying to take out her lipstick, "that's the way German men pick up girls. They give 'em names." She tried rouging her lips, but the cabbie made another sharp turn. "And Zola happens to be hard to say in German."

"Well, I've got news for you. Hedwig *ain't* any easier."

"You *haven't* been here long enough," Zola said, trying to powder her nose as the cabbie swerved the other way, "and when you live in a place long enough you get to know a lot of people, and I'm not ashamed of it."

"Whatever you say, Irmgard," as the taxi crashed into the bus ahead of them.

6

Unter den Linden

The Hotel Adlon bar, at 1 Unter den Linden, was known for its mural of mythic nudes high above the wood paneled bar. The head cocktail mixer, Franz dem Dicken, told everyone that the scene was from ancient times before the Armed Monks of the Sword had invaded the east. Dressed in a chemists' white smock and black tie, Franz dem Dicken placed a strainer over a silver mixer and poured Mr. Benchley and the Chicago foreign correspondent, Brayton Hills, a local version of the Tom Collins: The Betty Berlin. The two men raised their glasses and said, "Up your ass, Prohibition," knowing that the Germans understood not a word and that Calvin Coolidge could do nothing about the insult. A bar waiter promptly arrived and put slices of schinken, red cabbage, and knockwurst onto a white linen buffet table. Mr. Benchley put down his sketchbook, as he had been drawing the hotel bar, and said to Brayton Hills, "So, what did you come up with on the hotel mail theft?"

"Remember that explosion out on beyond the 12-mile limit, last January, in New York?"

"What about it?"

Brayton Hills said, "Two prominent bankers were listed on the death roll: Marbury Brush and Herston Bush. At first, I thought the latter's name was misspelled. Then I found out that Bush was connected to the Thyssen industrialist family over here. I got a hold of records of him staying in this hotel at the same exact time as one of the sons of the industrialist Thyssen. So, I double tipped the staff, and since everyone here is broke, they were more than willing to talk, and soon enough someone by the name of Egon von Remmele got into the picture and then someone else."

"Did you say von Remmele?"

"Yes, but you're pronouncing it the American way," Brayton Hills said."

"Well, I know someone with a similar sounding name. Now who's this von Remmele fella?"

"One of the most powerful industrialists in Germany, and Bush and Thyssen's elder son happen to be big supporters of the Austrian."

"You mean Hitler?"

"Yeah, the one whose insurrection miserably failed in '23, and it seems they all met here, including someone else, over several days, and there were some heated conversations.

"About what?"

"Politics, what else? And something crazy," Brayton Hills said.

"What?"

"I'll get to it in a second, but—"

"Who was the other person?"

"Emil Hugenberg."

"Who?"

Brayton Hills said, "Hugenberg was once on the board of Krupp Industries and he's the one who financed the conglomeration of all the rightwing newspapers in the provinces to create dissent against the Berlin press, which also feeds its news to all the provincial papers. You see, there's a battle of minds going on here and Hugenberg is trying to be the puppet master. The Berlin press is hated by the far right who hates the republic and anything democratic, and so Hugenberg's papers have carefully created an alternative narrative based on lies about the poisoning of German culture, which allegedly led to the loss of the war, which is anything but the truth, since the Germans just couldn't survive a war of attrition, especially when we got into it."

"And what about the Thyssen son?"

"He's one of those financially supporting the NSDAP, but he's not connected to the letter thefts, so we can forget about him for now."

"Why are they with Hitler's party?"

Brayton Hills said, "The NSDAP is better organized than all the other rightwing paramilitary groups and the Austrian is a good speaker. He knows how to communicate to people who suffer from the same grievances."

"You've heard him speak?"

"Yeah," Brayton Hills said, "and what he does well is to articulate those grievances into a voice that reassures people that something will be done about their anger, but he never says *how* other than to demonize the Jews into a vast conspiracy and then rant on about the purity and might of Aryan blood and the reawakening of Germany into a nation of single-minded men and women who will by magic end poverty, inequity, injustice, and hay fever, without of course dealing with the grim reality that people are looney, selfish, hypocritical, and downright mean when it comes to what they want and whom they'll blame or kill if they don't get it, and Hitler's all of that."

"Have you met him?"

"At a Munich beer garden and I asked him just how he was going to make Germany great again with all its problems, and he said that only he alone could do it, and I said, sure, but *how* are you going to do it? And he said by taking over the government and commanding industry and labor do to the things that people wanted, and I said what *you* want, and he said that that was one and the same thing. I reminded him that there's a lotta folks out there who don't want what you want; and he ended the interview. Afterwards, I was told that you don't ask Hitler questions, you just listen to him. And when I said that's not an interview, I was told that's what it is to him."

"And just how much of Germany is behind him?"

"Very little at the moment," Brayton Hills said. "A lot of folks just can't stand him, including those on the right. But the key to gaining power here, or anywhere else, is knowing how to bypass those people who don't like you."

"And just how do you do that?"

"By slowly expanding your coalition," Brayton Hills said, "until you reach the tipping point when everyone else steps in line like lemmings, because that's what people really are, though they would never admit it."

"And how close is he to that?

"Well," Brayton Hills said, "if the Dawes Plan succeeds and the economy continues to grow, you can say goodbye to Hitler and all those lunatics who want to bring down the Republic and create a single state with a dictator like Mussolini or Stalin."

"Is the Weimar Republic up to the challenge?"

"Let me put it this way," Brayton Hills said. "They're a bunch of snowflakes who would rather be weak and right than strong and wrong. They don't understand that weakness not only reinforces their perception of ineptitude, but is also the source of the debilitating infighting that disallows them to form a unified coalition inside the government, but with the Dawes Plan the government now believes that it can deliver, and who knows? Maybe I'm wrong. Maybe bullets will melt when fired."

Mr. Benchley said, "So, what does this letter that everyone is after have to do with all this?"

"Addison Prevette."

Mr. Benchley looked up from his sketchbook. "You know him?"

"Yeah, and a certain paramilitary group, within the Black Reichswehr, involved with Hugenberg, needs a letter of release concerning a shipment."

"Of what?"

"Arms."

"For another Putsch?"

"Or what we call an insurrection," Brayton Hills said. "You see, the nationalists believe that if the Dawes Plan succeeds it will put an end to any hopes of doing away with the democratic republic and reinstalling a monarchy or a dictatorship, depending upon which faction you talk to, since they like to end every sentence with a bullet."

"What about Addison Prevette?

Brayton Hills said, "He took over the Brush investment banking firm right after the death of Marbury Brush and one of the firm's clients happens to have been the late Ellis Remley, a pal of Emil Hugenberg."

"You mean Sarah Remley's late husband. And, so, she's related to this von Remmele fella?"

"Certainly not by spelling …I'd like to meet her, Bob."

"You will," Mr. Benchley said, "but are you saying that Addison Prevette is now involved with the Black Reichswehr."

"Well, his late partner Marbury Brush was."

"But you think—"

"I don't know what to think at this point," Brayton Hills said.

"Where's this shipment now?"

"The port of Hamburg," Brayton Hills said, "but the militants need that letter of release, and they'll kill to get it."

"And that's why you want to meet Sarah Remley?"

"Well, I also hear that she's beautiful……"

7

Himmel u. Hölle Kabarett

O r in English the Heaven and Hell Cabaret located on Berlin's grand Kurfürstendamm. Shelby could barely make out the sign as the rain blurred the taxi's window—not the same taxi that had crashed into the bus. She said to Zola, "You're sure you made reservations? Because I don't want to have to go looking for another cab in this weather."

"Don't worry, miss," Beau said. "I made 'em and iffen there be any problem gettin' in I'll speak to the boys in the jazz orchestra. They'll get us through because I have to get in," showing her his saxophone case.

Zola said to her cousin, "And you'll love what's on the program tonight,"

"What?"

"Spanking," Zola said, eyes full of mischief, as a strange looking man in an ill-fitting tuxedo opened the taxi door. He bowed and swept his arm and said to Zola, "What's your specialty, miss?"

"What's yours?"

"Riding you with a whip in hand," he said.

Zola ignored him and headed into the cabaret with Beau and Shelby tagging along.

The man in the bad tux got in front of Zola and said. "*Hey*, I remember you."

"Well, I don't remember you. Now outta my way."

"You're that American girl from 11 Giesebrechtstraße."

"Never heard of it," Zola said, trying to get past him.

"Madame Kitty's place," he said. "I used to work there serving drinks to the clients."

Zola ignored him. Shelby didn't. "How's the Major?" he said to Zola.

"Never heard of him," Zola lied as she entered the cabaret with Shelby and Beau in tow.

Shelby said to Zola, "Who's Madame Kitty?"

Zola said, "He's talking about Kitty Morton from Greenwich Village."

"No, he isn't……"

There were two big rooms inside the cabaret. On the right was Heaven and to the left was Hell. Zola took Shelby to where soaring flames of curtain strips streamed from an airflow of hidden fans. Waiters hustled in and out of the blaze dressed as pixie demons with fetching rods that had pointed ends for prodding into customers' behinds, mostly the females', and one of them belonged to Shelby. She searched for the culprit, but there were too many.

Then someone in a dinner jacket, white tie, and slicked back hair, guided them to their table. As they made their way through the crowd, Shelby noticed a young woman sitting on a grand piano. She wore only a teddy and was immersed in the dreamy things as she dangled a riding crop in one hand and sniffed from a little silver box in the other.

Shelby nudged her cousin. "One of your friends?"

"Unlike you, Miss Snob, everyone is my friend," Zola said as they sat down.

"Yeah, well, who was the one in the dinner jacket who brought us to this table—Dracula?"

"No, Siegfried, or better known as Ziggy," Zola said.

Ziggy returned to the table and sat down next to Zola and said, in German, "Long time no see. What happened to you?"

"I had to visit home," Zola said, "but I'm back."

"And who's your beautiful friend?"

"My friend is my cousin," Zola said. "I see the resemblance."

"I don't see any at all," Shelby said in German.

Siegfried laughed and said, "Then you've come to the right place."

Shelby, not sure what Ziggy meant, said in English to Zola, "Another one of your old friends?"

"I have a lot of old friends and hopefully you will too one day." Zola then turned to the girl in the teddy who took another sniff. "One of your new toys, Ziggy?"

"I wish. By the way, a lot has changed since you were last in Berlin, but you always seem to come back at the right moment." Ziggy pushed a silver snuff box across the table and let Zola put nose to powder.

"It all looks the same to me," Zola said.

Ziggy said, "You'll find out soon enough. And mainlining is better. Gets right to you, but etiquette disallows that unless you can find Gunther."

Zola pushed the snuff box toward her cousin and said, "Take some. It's like drinking wine, but without having to pee later." Shelby put nose to powder. Soon everything turned dreamy and soft including the Hades River waiters with their black iron cauldrons that they carried from table to table. One of them pulled out a bottle of champagne and something else that he waved at Shelby. Zola whispered in her ear, "He wants to spank you......"

8

Hotel Aldon Bar

Sarah entered the Aldon bar as Mr. Benchley and Brayton Hills were on their way out. Mr. Benchley said to her, "I was ready to give up on you."

Sarah looked around the bar that was now filled with evening drinkers. "Where is it quiet?"

Brayton Hills said, "Come with me."

They stepped into a grand hallway of Roman pillars and carved leaf ceiling medallions that led to the grand salon where they took a table in the far end corner.

"I thought maybe it was the weather keeping you," Mr. Benchley said, sitting down last.

"Not at all," Sarah said. "My cousin had invited me to his home for a family visit."

"You mean Egon von Remmele?"

"Yes, how did you know?"

Mr. Benchley turned to Brayton hills.

Sarah said, "Well, he wasn't there, but someone by the name of Hugenberg was."

"You mean Emil Hugenberg," Brayton Hill said, as he waved the waiter away.

"Yes."

"What did he want?"

"You know him?"

"Of him."

"Well, he wants to overthrow the government," Sarah said.

"He told you that?"

"In so many words," Sarah said, "and he even thought that I was there to help him."

"And just how would you be helping him?"

Sarah said, "He and my late husband were acquaintances, and somehow he assumed that I was part of their scheming—but he doesn't think that anymore."

"Too bad," Brayton Hills said. "Why?"

"Because if you had his trust then you could get more information out of him."

Sarah said, "Getting trust out of a man who mistrusts everything, including logic, isn't easy."

"Yes, but he's one of the most powerful men in Germany."

"Maybe," Sarah said, "but his kind of nonsense has no power over me."

"But when nonsense and power merge," Brayton Hills said, "it's no longer nonsense, but a problem, and overthrowing the government isn't a joke, as there've been two attempted insurrections already. Just what did he want from you?"

"He assumed that I was in possession of a certain letter," Sarah said. "Which letter?"

"One from my late husband."

"Do you have it?"

"The question is," Sarah said, "why does he want it so badly and at this very moment?

"Because," Brayton Hills said, "the right is worried that the Americans will save the Weimar Republic and, should that happen, the old conservative elite will never again rise to the height of power they had before the war in conjunction with the monarchy."

"And what power was that?" Sarah said.

"The power to, if not control, heavily influence industry and the government," Brayton Hills said.

"Yes, but what did my late husband have to do with all this?"

"Do you have the letter?"

"I have something else," Sarah said to Brayton Hills as she reached for the cloisonné lapel pin that she had found on her cousin's desktop. She set it on the table top the way a jeweler does to a prospective buyer.

Brayton Hills held it up to the light and said, "So, your cousin is now in with them."

"I have no idea whether he is, or he isn't."

Brayton Hills said, "The symbol on this membership pin is called a Hakenkreuz or swastika in English.

"That I know," Sarah said, "but why was Emil Hugenberg there and not my cousin?"

Brayton Hills handed her back the lapel pin and said, "We're going to find out."

Sarah said, "Seems my little vacation is turning into something else……"

9

It's Toasted

The Forde-Werke sedan left Grunewald via the Koenigs Allee under heavy rainfall. Passing cars were seen as headlights only. Major von Coors, sitting in the backseat with Emil Hugenberg, held out a Lucky Strike *50's* tin and said, "American cigarettes. Try one."

"…What's wrong with German cigarettes?"

"Nothing, but Lucky's are toasted," the Major said, showing Emil Hugenberg the tin.

"I've never heard of a toasted cigarette."

"No one has. It's bullshit," the Major said, "including the claim that toasting tobacco makes Lucky Strike cigarettes less irritating on the throat, but then that's the deviousness of the American mind, Herr Hugenberg, and there's something to learn from it. When you pontificate in your newspapers about our cause, you bore the readers to death with your long-winded articles. But we're going to change all that by using short catchy phrases and images to provoke discontent that can then be turned into a rallying cry to rid Germany of all its vermin."

"You will also distance yourself from a lot of people."

"The only people who think that are people like you who never served."

"I was too old to serve in the war and you know that."

"And if you were young, you'd have said that you had bone spurs in your feet." The Major then held out his buckskin gray gloved hand. "The letter of release, please."

"Major, you're no angrier than I am about the outcome of the war, but we lost it because of the English naval blockade and the millions of Americans pouring into France. I say that as a realist not as a defeatist."

"Herr Hugenberg, the Americans had no idea what the fuck they were doing. They got lost on the way over."

"Yes, but if a man learns that he has cancer, he doesn't do so because it pleases him."

The Ford-Werke swerved away from a passing car as it turned into the Kurfürstendamm. The Major said, "Give me the letter of release."

"…There was a slight hitch," Emil Hugenberg said.

"A what…?"

"The American woman."

"Herr Hugenberg—"

"She insisted that she knew nothing of the letter."

"Herr Hugenberg, a woman does not sail across the Atlantic Ocean right after her husband dies just to see the Berlin Zoo elephants."

"She's a difficult woman, Major."

"She gave it to von Remmele?"

"Well, he was there, of course," Emil Hugenberg lied, "and he tried everything but strangling her, but she wouldn't budge."

"That's because you're a sissy."

"I *told* you; the woman was very difficult."

"Because you're a sissy."

"I'm *not* a sissy. And I *told* you; I'll get it later on tonight."

"Maybe you're planning on selling it."

"Maybe you should've gone for the letter yourself."

"Had I, I wouldn't have been a sissy and let a woman take advantage of me."

"Major, she took advantage of my decency, not my manhood."

"Maybe you have a thing for her."

"Don't be stupid, Major."

"Maybe you're no match for her."

"When a woman forgets her place, she is no longer a woman."

"Did she bite you?"

"Of course not," Emil Hugenberg said, "but she made comments that between men would have started a war and that's a shame, because she is beautiful and still young enough to be had, though to anyone with manhood she's utterly sexless once she opens her mouth."

The Ford-Werke sedan pulled up to the Heaven and Hell Cabaret. The Major stepped out and said, "Herr Hugenberg, I want that letter by midnight."

"I'll have it for you in the morning."

"You'll have it by *midnight*."

"Major, you were on the boat with Sarah Remley from New York. You had all the time in the world to get the letter, but you didn't."

"And for the simple reason that *you*, Herr Hugenberg, not I, was designated as the recipient. Now, you will get me that letter by midnight, or you'll regret having played games with me."

Emil Hugenberg leaned into the Major and said, "*Don't* you threaten me, young man."

"Be glad that's all I've done……"

10

Perverts

Ilse Dietrich shut the door of her dressing room in the Heaven and Hell Cabaret and then sat down at her maquillage table. She uncapped her fountain pen, checked the level of ink, and began to write.

Anna Raeder
135 Chrystie Street, 3A
Lower East Side, New York, USA

Dear Anna
Everyone on the Lower East Side is talking about how badly I'm doing here—wherever "here" is—and that's why you're getting this letter to straighten things out once and for all about where I am *not*. Now, in some ways, yeah, I'm doing lousy. But then everyone is doing lousy even when everything seems to be sailing along like when I was an A student in college and my father said to me: 'All the other girls are getting married and are no longer burdens to their fathers, but sadly I got a kid who doesn't understand the value of money and I'm not made out of it'. So, I said to him, 'For someone who's supposed to understand the value of money, why the hell are you always broke?' He hit me for the last time. So, I scrammed for good. And let me tell you this: if someone is a buzzard, it matters not that he's your

father—decency is something earned not inherited.

Now about that ridiculous gossip in your letter. *No,* I did not leave home, because I was pregnant, and *I did not shoot* that Prohibition agent even though I was two feet away from him at the Murray Hill speakeasy when gunfire broke out last December. And if you should run into any of the old gang, which I know you will two minutes after reading this letter, because you'll be on the telephone reciting every word of it— just make sure that you tell blabbermouth Emily Fischbein, that zaftig with the Goldilocks perm, that she *did not* steal my boyfriend, because I had four of them when I left New York and all she could get was the dumbest one and I hope she has to marry him and scrub his kitchen floor for the rest of her life and bring him his pipe and slippers for the rest of her life and pick up his clothing for the rest of her life and scrub it with her hands until they're dried out like my mother's.

Now that you've got the lay of the land concerning my whereabouts, I need you to do me a very special favor, because you're a very reliable person and that's a quality that I know you would never want to jeopardize. There happens to be a famous speakeasy in Greenwich Village called Barney Gallant's (the one you've been dying to get in!) and they never allow just anyone inside, only the cream of the crop. But you're in luck. Barney is my favorite cousin (he's obviously on my mother's side), and all you have to do is tell him that I'm in a city that has a lot of Platz's and that's why I can no longer have lunch with him on Wednesdays in that spaghetti joint over on Bleecker Street. Tell him that I've been sending him letters, but I got wise from a secret source that the feds steal all his mail so they can build a case against him and lock him up again for selling hooch. Now, all you have to do is go over to his speak on 40 Washington Square South and give him my address that's inside the sealed envelope that I'm sending you that you *better not* open. And if you make a good impression on him, he might even allow you into his club and then you'll be popular like no one else in the world. Other than that, I miss you and the Polo Grounds and that guy in the bleachers who use to sell us rum for half price because of our feminine charms—too bad he was a shaygetz.

Yours truly,
Rachel (I'll be using my middle name, Ilse, from now on to steer clear of the damn Prohis.)

Ilse heard a knock on her dressing room door and hid the letter. She said in flawless German, "*Whaddya* want?"

Oskar, her servant, reminded her, "It's getting close to show time, Mistress Ilse, and some gentlemen have sent you more champagne from Heaven. They say that they're now on the way over to Hell to see you."

"Yeah, well, tell 'em to go to hell."

"Yes, Mistress Ilse. Should I stay by the door until you need me?"

"What I need I can never get."

"Yes, Mistress Ilse…Have you considered the proposal?"

"Is that why you're at the door?"

"Only to serve you, Mistress Ilse."

"…Alright. Come on in."

Oskar entered, eyes to the floor. Ilse was buck naked except for the cigarette in her hand. She turned away from her maquillage mirror to see if he was looking at her. He wasn't. She said, "I've considered the proposal."

"You have, Mistress Ilse?"

"Yes," Ilse said, walking across the dressing room, her dark red flowing bob framing her intense blue eyes that distanced anyone who dared more than to look at her. "You have certainly proven to be a good servant, but this request of yours needs to be well considered, before permission is granted. Now, you've been with me for a while and you've proven to be punctual, tidy, and well mannered. I assume that you will continue to be so as there has been no indication, as of yet, that any inner conflicts will sabotage all the good work that you've done. Having said that, and maybe at some risk, I agree to allow you to dress me, but if I find out that you're a pervert and are doing it for some dirty pleasure, you'll be dismissed and punished. Remember that you are only allowed to touch me as a consequence of the action of dressing me, and nothing else. We are strictly business here. We have our functions. We have purpose. And we rise above the petty impulses."

"Yes, Mistress Ilse, and I will wear gloves to reduce any of kind improper transmission to my fingertips."

"Well, I think you're nuts, but…permission to dress me is granted." Oskar put on his gloves and got to work.

11

Backstage

The Hell showgirls, some barely dressed, some not at all, crowded the red brick hallway under the vapor of makeup light and cigarette smoke. Ziggy squeezed through and knocked on the door of the only private dressing room in the cabaret and then, without waiting for an answer she opened it, and said in German to Shelby, "Meet the Voodoo Child."

Ilse, now dressed in a red leather corset and matching red leather boots up to her thighs, told Oskar to leave. She then took a long look at Shelby and said in English, "So…you came looking for me."

Ziggy said in German, as she spoke no English, "You know each other?"

Ilse said to her, "How long are you two going to stay?" meaning the couch in the corner.

"Long enough," Ziggy said.

Shelby, now out of her fog, said in English, "*You're* the Voodoo Child?"

Ilse ignored her.

Shelby said, "You had another name when you were arrested."

Ziggy said to Ilse, "What's she talking about?"

"Leave us alone for a second," Ilse said.

"I will not, and what's going on here?"

"I know her from home," Ilse lied. "We need a moment to talk. I haven't spoken to another American in ages."

"That's the best thing you ever did," Ziggy said.

"Just give us a few minutes. We're old friends," Ilse lied.

Ziggy eyed them both and said, "A few minutes, but that's all. And no funny stuff; she's mine," and left.

Ilse, at five-feet-four, walked around Shelby who was two inches shorter. "Who told you I was here?"

"No one did," Shelby said.

"You got your letter back. What else do you want?"

"Nothing," Shelby said.

"So, you just happened to walk on in here."

"I'm here like everyone else, for a good time."

"*That* I believe."

There was a hard knock on the door from the stage assistant who said, "Second bell, Ilse."

Ilse yelled, "I'll be right out."

Shelby said to her, "If you're the Voodoo Child, why did you have to steal my letter?"

"Look," Ilse said, "you got your letter. The couch is over there. When the show is over, you two better be done."

"What're you talking about?"

"Whaddya think?"

"I don't know what to think," Shelby said, foggy from the powder. "Look, why don't we meet up after the show?"

"I'm busy," Ilse said.

"We could have breakfast at my hotel, then."

"Look, Ziggy doesn't share her pets with anyone."

"What're you talking about?"

"You heard me."

"I'm *not* his pet"

"You mean *her* pet," Ilse said.

"*Her* pet?"

"Ziggy's a woman."

"He is?"

"No, *she* is, and she brought you here for a particular reason, and don't tell me that you didn't know."

"I *didn't* know, and it was my cousin who brought me here," Shelby said.

"Then what're you doing with Ziggy, or did she pick you up outside?"

"My cousin knows her," Shelby said.

"Who's your cousin?"

"Zola Nicholas."

"…Zola? With a Southern accent like yours?"

"Yeah, you *know* her?"

"Is she the one who goes by the name of Lipstick?"

"Yeah," Shelby said, "but how do you know her?"

"I ran into her in New York."

"She never told me that."

"Not my fault," Ilse said.

"How come everyone knows her over here?"

"She's got a reputation," Ilse said, pointing to the couch in the corner and then heading to the door.

"What do you mean she's got a reputation?"

"Whaddya think?"

"I don't know what to think."

"Well, think harder," Ilse said.

"What kind of reputation are you talking about?"

"She's a pro-skirt."

"If it's what I think it is, then it's a lie," Shelby said.

"It's the truth. Now, I've got a show to do."

"My cousin is *not* a whore."

"If that's what you wanna believe," Ilse said.

"You shouldn't say things about people that aren't true."

"Then you've got a lot to learn."

"What do you mean I've got a lot to learn?"

Isle opened the door of her dressing room and stared at the beautiful girl who was as angry as she was confused. "…What time do you eat breakfast?"

"Eight o'clock," Shelby said.

Ilse heard the last call. "What's your room number?"

"Same one where you stole my letter."

Günther removed the syringe from under the table. Shelby took notice of his hand as the Major pulled out a chair for her. She took the one beside her cousin instead, and said to her in English, "I need to talk to you about something," but Zola was too far gone.

The Major said to Shelby in German, "How was your little visit to the dressing room?"

Shelby ignored him and kept her eyes on Beau who was playing in the jazz orchestra.

"You two were rather quick," the Major said.

"You're rather slow," Shelby said, reaching for a matchstick.

The Major struck one for her. "Why are you so nasty?"

Shelby ignored him.

"Fräulein Prevette, when a gentleman offers you a chair, you say thank you, even if you don't want it."

"When a *gentleman* does."

"Fräulein," the Major said, leaning into her, "I bear your company because you're Zola's cousin."

"If it's too much to bear then leave."

"Young lady, you do not talk to a man as if you are one."

"Herr von Coors, if I threaten you, then you're no man."

The Major ignored her. "I see you like nigger music."

Shelby ignored him.

"The idiots can't even play together. They sound more like a bunch of morons arguing with each other.

"You're the idiot, Major. Jazz has taken over the world—something that you'll never do."

"Dear Fraulein, what you need is for me to pull up your step-in and give you a good hot spanking."

"Fuck off."

"And a washing out of your mouth, too."

Shelby turned to Zola for help, but she was out of it. The Major, enjoying Shelby's discomfort, said, "But then, of course, you've never really listened to Wagner, Bach, or Beethoven, because if you had, then you'd understand that not having niggers in one's country protects its culture from getting vulgarized."

"You have them right over there," Shelby said, pointing to the orchestra.

"They won't be here for long."

"And just what do you plan on doing? Shoot them all?"

"Thank you for the suggestion," the Major said.

"That wasn't a suggestion; it was a conclusion."

"Fräulein, you're a Southerner, and I know your people feel the same way about the nigger problem as we do over here."

"Then why is every cabaret in Berlin begging for a black jazz orchestra?"

"Fräulein, that's because jungle music was brought here for our amusement as were the monkeys in the zoo."

"So, now we're in a zoo."

"It's getting to be one."

"And you're the main attraction," Shelby said.

The Major put his mouth over her ear. Shelby felt his spit as he said, "You're a nasty little girl, Fräulein, and if we were alone, I'd punish you."

Pushing him away, Shelby said, "Major, if we were alone, it would be punishment enough."

The lights then dimmed as Hell slowly turned into a fiery glow. A leg amputee appeared onstage, unshaven, wearing a ragged cloth cap and a worn wool jacket with an Iron Cross 1st class pinned to it. He carried a stool and placed it behind a harmonium. Once he secured himself, he put hand to key and played, in lento, the opening notes of the German national anthem, *Das Lied der Deutschen,* and layered each note so that the sound expanded into an eerie dirge filling the cabaret. The Voodoo Child then appeared under a soft light which followed her as she slowly made her way toward the audience that voiced itself in fits across the room. She waited them out and only then did she commence to sing the Lied in a raw voice that demilitarized the official version and reset it into the intimacy of grief and all that was lost in the madness of the war, and for this they loved her, as did the Major.

12

Front Row Seats

The morning sun whitewashed the third-floor apartment of 11 Giesebrechtstraße. Zola was in one of its rooms, face down on a bed, dress pushed back, wrists bound, bottom bare. She gripped the bedsheet in her hands and with clenched teeth said, "*Harder......*"

Later, Madame Kitty said to Zola, over coffee in the parlor of the apartment, "You just all of a sudden vanished."

"I...I had to go home," Zola said, as she fixed her hair and straightened out her dress.

"Because of that boy?"

"I'd rather not talk about him," Zola said, trying not to think of Bartel Pschorr.

Kitty then handed her an envelope filled with German marks. Zola said, "You never paid this much."

"You can thank the Dawes Plan."

Zola took the cash and turned to the Major who was waiting in the hallway. "Did you hear that?" She then hurried out, as she was already late.

Ilse Dietrich was in the Hotel Adlon's tea room, where high living was never rushed and politeness always overruled disagreeableness, and if you disagreed the staff was brought out.

She was hiding under a Lucie Hamar hunter green wool cloche that was pulled down over her eyes. Zola strolled up to the table and said, "Enjoying fame?" meaning all the stares that Ilse was getting from the crowded room.

"Not as much as you mine," Ilse said. "And you're late."

"I got tied up," Zola said, gladly taking in an eye that fell upon her before moving back to Ilse. "Must be fun being famous."

"How would you know?"

"I just did for a moment," Zola said, finding the chair a bit hard on her bottom. "Now, what's so important that you've exposed yourself to the world?"

"We need to talk about something."

"If you mean the Major," Zola said, "he just told me about the speech that you're going to give at the Hofbrauhaus am Platzl, and he's scared that you'll take over his movement once everyone hears you, which I find very amusing—*if* you know what I mean."

"I don't."

"You're a Jewess."

"Maybe you should tell him."

"I'm just making a point," Zola said, "not a judgment."

"And just how do you separate the two?"

"Look," Zola said, "I was engaged to a Hebrew who just happened to have been your late cousin Bartel Pschorr from Grunewald."

"Falling in love is not moral courage."

"I didn't say it was."

"You didn't have to. It was implied."

"Look, you're the one who invited me here," Zola said, pouring herself a cup of tea and grabbling several butter biscuits. "Now, what can I do for you?"

"Have you had any contact with my family, since you've been here?"

"If you mean Manfred Pschorr, no," Zola said, "and I think you can understand why."

"Human nature precedes logic."

"Exactly," Zola said.

"And for that alone, I doubt that you came all the way back to Berlin to write silly magazine stories about silly society people."

"Actually, I find it very amusing," Zola said, crunching on a biscuit, "especially those who have power."

"Then you're in luck."

"…How's that?"

Ilse said, "I want you to write about the treachery and deceit of certain powerful people who are hell bent on destroying this country by use of bogus patriotism and lies to consolidate political power."

"Well, if there's been a revolution here, I missed it."

"Then you never read a history book," Ilse said.

"I'm an American. What do I care about history?"

"If you like being dumb, fine. And just what do you see in the Major, anyway?"

"Not what you think," Zola said.

"What should I think?"

"Look," Zola said, "the Hun and I, for some crazy reason, get along, and don't ask me why, but it's nothing intimate."

"What is it then?"

"We're playmates," Zola said, "which is a little different."

"Whatever it is," Ilse said, "you now have a unique opportunity to expose the Major and all the other dumbass paramilitary groups for what they really are. But to do that, you'll need someone on the inside who can give you access to those people in power to get the real story."

"I already know the Major."

"You'll need more than that clown," Ilse said.

"Who else then…?"

"Manfred Pschorr, you late fiancé's father." Ilse said. "I just spoke to him, and he wants to let bygones be bygones, so that you can write about the diabolical forces at work here."

"I thought your side of the family was estranged."

"Not anymore," Ilse said. "My cousin picked up a copy of *Die Dame* magazine and recognized me from the pictures that my father had sent to my grandmother whom I've never met. But getting back to the point of why you're here, besides eating all the butter biscuits, he wants you to do a series of articles in *The New Yorker* magazine about the titanic battle going on over here between good and evil which America will want to take sides on. He also thinks that it will be a damn good warning of what will happen to us, if we don't watch it down the road."

"You're asking a lot," Zola said.

"See at it as a way of making yourself famous."

"Yeah, but I don't think that the average American gives a hoot about what happens over here."

"Make them."

"Good luck," Zola said."

"Why don't you tell your editor about the idea? He might like it," Ilse said.

"He's already got Robert Benchley doing the political stuff."

"Yeah, but it'll have more impact coming from a woman."

"You mean it will have *less* impact," Zola said. "Woman journalists are confined to the home section of newspapers and magazines. That's why my job is not politics, just speakeasies and cabarets; and I can assure you, there's no way that I'm going to jeopardize my current job and end up in the home section of some newspaper in Wichita writing about linoleum for the modern woman—and by the way, are you going to the transvestite's ball tonight?"

"Why?"

Zola got up and said, "Someone told me that the Major is coming dressed as a woman, which I find *really* hard to believe."

"You're pals with him," Ilse said. "Why don't you ask him?"

"I did. Said he wouldn't be caught dead at a faggot party."

"Well, as long as he's stays alive, he won't have to worry."

Zola reached over and took the last biscuit. "Thanks for the tea, and don't worry; I won't tell anyone that you're a Jewess."

Ilse looked up from her cloche and said, "When people say that, I begin to worry......"

13

Grunewald, Berlin

The Major took a taxi to the Grunewald hunting lodge and was led into the library by the footman. Egon turned away from the big window that faced the Grunewaldsee and offered the Major a drink and his choice of tobacco. The Major lit up a cigarette and sat back into his chair. "You should've seen Ilse last night."

Egon said, "I saw her the other night at my dinner party."

"Yeah, but to see her perform is another thing, and it's about time that you did, because she can take the simplest line and fill it with meaning that makes you one with her. Especially if she's feeling sad or betrayed or injured—you want to stand by her and fight against those who have done her harm and that's something that we need: a spokesman like her."

"What exactly did she say?"

"It's how she said it."

"What did she say?"

"She didn't say anything," the Major said. "What she did, this time, was to sing our national anthem."

"Is that what they're doing in cabarets now?"

"It's what the Voodoo Child did."

"That's not exactly cabaret music," Egon said.

"That's why she's a genius."

"Well," Egon said, "I'll look into it, but that's not why I invited you here."

"I was getting to that."

"And I think it's important for everyone to be on the same page," Egon said."

"Which page is that?"

"Maybe I wasn't clear the other night at the dinner party," Egon said.

"Maybe not, but the Austrian was having a hell of a time. He was all over Ilse, once again."

"That's another issue, but I'm more concerned, now, with the politische Kampfbünde"

"Why…?"

"Because," Egon said, "these combat leagues are organizing the local population, not for any coming insurrection, but to achieve the political goals for when the time does come."

"Since when did you give a shit about political indoctrination and not just money?"

Egon absorbed the insult. "Major…the object is to teach everyone, especially our youth, how to get back to nature through group activities, such as soldiering, though we wouldn't call it that, and to emphasize the group over the self, the leader over everyone else, and that deep bond between blood and soil, as those cultural organizations did—without any political leadership—back in the 1890s. Our aim now is to create a new society, prior to obtaining power, which will be able to function from day one, unlike the Soviets who had to start from scratch and will end up there."

"Well, it's nice to know what you and that dumb shit Austrian are doing," the Major said.

"Major…your notion of blunt force is long over. Times have changed and so must you."

"I've heard all that before," the Major said, "but if you think some jackass corporal from Austria is equal to any aristocrat—we, who built this country of science and industry that all the world envies and comes to by the droves to learn from—then we might as well get a donkey to lead this country."

"You're missing the point, Major."

"No, you are."

"Major, I've *heard* him speak."

"Good for you."

Egon said, "When you create a movement you need an individual who can embody it with his voice or you have a lot of voices, which leads to lot of noise."

"You're telling me that I can't speak?"

"Major, I'm saying that you have an excellent mind, but on the podium no wants to listen to a man with a high-pitched voice."

"Well, if it comes down to a popularity contest," the Major said, "then we're all fucked."

"Find someone who can speak, Major. There must be someone out there. Then come back to me, but you better hurry because many already believe that they have found their savior."

"That shitfaced Austrian…?"

"Yes, that shitfaced Austrian, but then people go to church not because they believe in God, but because the alternative is worse. You must give people an alternative."

The Major stood up and said to his host, "Never allow a man from the gutter to lead a nation, or he will take it back into the gutter. And being able to speak to the masses doesn't mean that you know what's best for them; you're just speaking for them and what they want, which means that you don't know what the hell you want, either. The great men of the past weren't necessarily great speakers, instead they built the greatest industrial nation ever, only to be sold out at the last moment by a bunch of shitfaced bureaucrats and working-class idiots who will accept any promise thrown at them. And if you so much as allow yourself to be seduced by this little shit Hitler, then we're all doomed. He's from the gutter and will take us there because that's where he's most comfortable."

"Major…just because I've made contact with his people, doesn't mean that I've disowned you."

"You *joined* their party and left ours," the Major said.

"I still belong to your party."

"You're hedging your bets."

"Major, what you don't understand is that I'll have influence over the little Austrian. *I* hold the purse strings. We'll both control him."

"Well, if you want to play pin the donkey with that Austrian weasel then you better understand that a strong man from the gutter has no room for anyone but himself and that's his weakness, and like a wound it will always be sore to anything that goes near it. He will reason, by that alone, and that alone is reason enough to avoid him. Everything that he will do will *not* be in the interest of the nation, but in his own interest, based on his immediate needs. His survival is what consumes him and nothing else. On the other hand, we aristocrats are born to authority and are obliged by the responsibility that comes with it. This little shit Austrian is nothing but a street clown who once thought that he could paint and now thinks that he can take on the world, but beware—when the paint dries and the image fades, so will he."

"For once you make sense, Major," Egon said, getting up and taking the Major gently by the arm, "and that is why we must be seen as constitutionally minded men, otherwise we'll be deemed as illegitimate. Once in power, we can do what we want with the former corporal and the opposition. But you are *not* to take that shipment of arms. You are *not* to try to overthrow the government. You will forfeit not only the movement, but everything that you and I have worked for all these years."

The Major headed to the door and said, "Well, since I don't have the letter of release, I don't think you need to worry."

But Egon did.

14

Home Sweet Home

Ethel Wundermacher
130 Orchard Street, 3B
Lower East Side, New York, USA

Dear Ethel,

I just got your letter this afternoon and I'm really trying to figure out what's going on in your head, because anyone with a brain knows that when a girl gets married and four hours after the ceremony, she realizes that she made a big mistake and then runs away and finds herself on Orchard Street with another boy whom she had just met at a vaudeville show on Delancey Street where she'd been hiding, she really needs to think things over. Nevertheless, Agnes Klugherz, who works at Eckstein's over on Orchard Street, once told me that you have to be married for at least twenty-four hours for it to be legit, unless of course you've already dropped your drawers. But if they do hunt you down and find you, I am now thinking that you may really be in trouble, because once you're married, according to the vow at least, you're married forever, and if that is true, then get used to ironing, cleaning, and serving your husband's every whim, because I don't think you've got a chance of being a school teacher once they find out that you're 'lacking in morals' for leaving your husband. And forget about being a lawyer. Only a man could get away with dumping his wife and making millions while also being a snake. And that's why no one can find me.

Love, Rachel

Oskar knocked on the bedroom door. Ilse opened it and walked him over to the window and pointed down into the street. "Do you know who that man is wearing the Homburg? Because he's been there every day."

Oskar looked out and said, "I have no idea, Mistress Ilse. But I'll chase him away if you wish."

"Please do, and make sure he stays away."

Ilse then stepped away from the window and gave the radiator another kick. "What about the heating? It's still not working, and I've got to be at the Hotel Esplanade for breakfast."

"I thought the Major was coming to see you, Mistress Ilse."

"The hell with him. Now, what about the heating?"

"Someone is attending to the problem right now, Mistress Ilse, and he informed me that it should be fixed, soon enough." Oskar handed her a large cream-colored envelope that was sealed with blue priority wax. "This was just delivered, Mistress Ilse."

Ilse closed her floral velvet burnout dressing gown and opened the invitation. "Oh, this is for the transvestite ball tonight."

"Have you decided on what you'll be wearing, Mistress Ilse?"

She walked over to her armoire. "I was thinking black tie and top hat."

"Trousers of course."

"Of course."

"Men's shoes?"

"Only boys' will fit," Ilse said.

"And Siegfried?"

"I'm going with her brother."

"You mean with Major von Coors…?"

"He thinks I made a deal with him," Ilse said, as she searched her armoire and pulled out a black-tie outfit and held it against her chest. She reached inside a pocket for a monocle and put it to her eye.

Oskar said, "You look like a veritable industrialist, Mistress Ilse."

"Like hell I do."

"And what will the Major be wearing, Mistress Ilse?"

"Well, if he comes dressed as a man then he better be able to prove that he's a woman."

"There are straight men who like to wear women's attire," Oskar said.

"If you mean the Major, I have no idea. But he's coming dressed as a woman or else."

"Then it should be interesting, Mistress Ilse."

"It will be. He's not only going to wear a dress, but girls underwear too and everything else that goes with it. That's the deal."

"You seem to have him at your command, Mistress Ilse."

"Don't let *him* know that," she said.

"…Might I inquire as to what you did in America, before coming here?"

"I was in college."

"Studying what?"

"Psychology and getting all A's too, and Mrs. Whitman took me under her wing for a Doctor of Philosophy." Ilse dropped her robe. Oskar immediately turned away. She found a dress and stood before her full-length mirror and then pulled out another. "I once wrote a thesis about clothing as it relates to the art of seduction and the display of power with its coded fetishization, and Mrs. Whitman really loved it. The newspapers picked it up and my thesis was the talk of the town and all the top hats read it, and then everything went kaput."

"I didn't know that you were so educated, Mistress Ilse."

"You thought I was dumb?" Ilse said, pulling out another dress and holding it under her neck. "Now, take the Klan—"

"The who, Mistress Ilse?"

"Oh, they're a bunch of cracked eggs from back home who wear bedsheets they peed in the night before and give themselves horseshit names like Grand Dragon, but they use highly provocative symbols to express a group identity that never has to be spoken. No different than the Nazi Hakenkreuz."

"I've never thought of that," Oskar said.

"Well, now you can." She found another dress. "And human beings don't need to understand what something is, they just have to know how they feel, and to be with others who feel the same way. Verification by feeling, not by reasoning—anyway, I never did get that doctorate," Ilse said, looking for another dress. "Some cheapskate wanted me to marry a schlemiel and then refused to pay for spring semester, so I skedaddled."

The house bell rang. Oskar excused himself and left the bedroom. Rachel slipped on her robe and followed him out. She heard a man in the hallway say, "The heating unit in the basement is fixed, but I'll be back later on to see if it's still in order." He left the apartment as Rachel entered the foyer.

She said to Oskar, "Why was he wearing a uniform?"

"Because he's on his way to the rally, Mistress Ilse."

"Where?"

"One of those cheap beer halls."

"How do you know?"

"My brother's going with him......"

15

Hotel Esplanade

Ilse, out of breath, found Shelby at the top of the breakfast room stairs. "Sorry I'm late, but someone's been following me."

"Who?"

"Some button man in a Homburg," Ilse said.

"Why's he following you?

"I don't know. I took the lower stairway and then crossed over to lose him."

"Is he still here?"

"I hope not."

"Well, we can't stay here," Shelby said.

"Where do you wanna go?"

"Come on; we'll order breakfast in my room." They hurried to the service stairway.

Mr. Benchley opened the door to his room and said, "Polizei" to the two men trying to get into Sarah Remley's room right across from his. They stared at each other not sure if the man with the foreign accent was kidding or not and decided that he wasn't. They hurried down the hallway and passed Shelby and Ilse on their way up.

Mr. Benchley said to Shelby, "Those two men were trying to get into Mrs. Remley's room. I tried calling the house dick, but he never came."

He was on his way, now.

Mr. Benchley turned to him. "Kind of late, aren't you?"

The house dick ignored him and said to Ilse in German, "So, you're back again."

Shelby said, "Miss Dietrich is my guest, so you can't throw her out."

The house dick didn't care and said to Ilse, "Did the Bund Wiking send you over this time?"

Ilse said to him, "I've got nothing to do with them."

"Sure, you don't," he said and then to Mr. Benchley. "You the one who called the concierge?"

Shelby said, "He doesn't speak German."

The house dick said, "Well, what does he speak?"

"English," Shelby said.

"Something you should know if you work in a hotel," Ilse added.

The house dick took her by the arm. "I'm taking you in for violating a disassociation notice."

Mr. Benchley said to the house dick, "I'd like to have a word with you, sir."

The house dick said to Shelby, "What's buggin' him?"

"He wants to speak to you."

"How the hell can he do that, if he can't speak German?"

"I don't know," Shelby said. "Give it a try."

Mr. Benchley put some hard-to-get dollar bills into the house dick's pocket and said, "This is for minding your own business."

The house dick let go of Ilse's arm, but said to her, "Keep him around the next time you stop by, or you're gonna have a problem." He went on his way.

Mr. Benchley said to Shelby, "Have you seen Mrs. Remley?"

"No, I haven't."

"The concierge told me that she didn't pick up her key last night."

Ilse said to Mr. Benchley. "Did you say Remmele?"

"Yes," Mr. Benchley said. "Why?"

Ilse said, "Have you ever heard of Egon von Remmele?"

"In fact, I have," said Mr. Benchley.

Ilse said, "Then I'm not surprised that she's gone."

"Why's that?" Mr. Benchley said.

"Because Germany's like a trap door," Ilse said.

"How so?"

"There's nothing to stand on."

"And how do you know von Remmele?" Mr. Benchley said.

"I know a lot of people that I know nothing about."

"But you know him," Mr. Benchley said.

"Of him. That's all," Ilse said.

"Well, either way," Mr. Benchley said, and then to Shelby, "I'm late and have to run over to the Café Josty to meet Zola. I just received word from New York that our magazine wants us to head over to Paris, but I'm not going anywhere until we first sort things out over here." He then turned to Ilse. "Would you like to join us?"

Ilse noticed W.J. Herman's 1920 *What You Want to Say and How you Want to Say It - in German* phrasebook sticking out of Mr. Benchley's coat pocket and said, "You'll need more than that to sort things out over here……"

16

Café Josty

Trams, busses, and automobiles battled for space as they scurried around Potsdamer Platz, but Café Josty wasn't affected by the commotion as it was located on the widest part of the plaza where patrons could always be private in public as on the boulevards of Paris—unlike Manhattan.

Shelby took a window table and watched a double decker bus plastered with ads trundle by. Ilse took the seat beside her and said, "So, how did you get from Mississippi to Manhattan?"

"My family has friends there."

"In Berlin too?"

"No, I'm just on vacation," Shelby said. "What brought you here?"

"A pain in the neck did."

"Who?"

"A real cheapskate." Ilse turned to Mr. Mr. Benchley. "What about you?"

"As I said before, Zola and I work for the same magazine and we're doing a piece on Berlin. She's covering the nightlife. I'm doing the political side."

"And just how do you cover it when you can't speak German?"

"I have friends who give me all the information that I need… What can you tell me?"

"I don't know anything about politics," Ilse said.

"You know Magnus von Coors, the former Reichswehr officer and leader of the DNF. That's a pretty good start."

"That's what you think," Ilse said.

"What about the Bund Wiking?"

"What about it?"

"You tell me?"

"There's nothing to tell you," Ilse said. "So, then, how do you know the Major?"

"He's the brother of the woman who runs Der Himmel u. Hölle Kabarett.

"Do they know that Ilse Dietrich is a phony name?"

"…Just what're you getting at?"

"You know what I'm getting at," Mr. Benchley said. "You met Zola last January at a Manhattan speakeasy in Manhattan's Garment District. I read the profile that she wrote about you in *The New Yorker*. We tried to find you for a follow up, but you had already left the country."

"Well, *I* didn't read it."

"You should've" Mr. Benchley said. "And when we got to Berlin, Zola was more than surprised to find out that the sensation of Berlin was only a few months ago an American college girl from the Lower East Side of Manhattan, named Rachel Pschorr, whom she had interviewed in a Garment District speakeasy."

"We recently moved to the Bronx, but get to the point," Ilse said.

Mr. Benchley took out his sketch pad and began to draw both teenagers. He said, "You seem to have gone from nowhere to somewhere very quickly."

"What're you doing with that pencil?"

"I'm drawing."

"So, you can sell my image?"

"No, Rachel, to put it in my magazine for nothing. You see, there happen to be two 19-year-old American girls in Berlin who speak volumes about what a real flapper is in the long process of women's emancipation, not that silly stuff you see in Hollywood flickers, or read about in slick magazines, or in those I'm-going-to-faint novels, but if

Major von Coors should ever find out your real name—who you really are—it could be a bit of a problem for you."

"What kind of problem?"

Mr. Benchley said, "I think you know that Zola was once engaged to a wealthy young man from Grunewald, a suburb of Berlin, who was also a Hebrew."

"And…?"

"His name was Bartel Pschorr of the Pschorr shipping family, and you just happen to be his cousin."

"Why're you telling me this?"

"Pschorr ships throughout the world."

"I'm thrilled," Ilse said, wondering where the waiter was.

"The company can ship your car anywhere."

"I don't have a car," Ilse said to him.

"Your furniture too."

"Wonderful," Ilse said, checking her bag for a smoke.

"Guns too…"

Ilse looked up from her bag. "Just what are you getting at?"

"Do you see your cousins often?"

And just why do you want to know?"

The waiter arrived. Mr. Benchley waved him away. "It has to do with that letter you stole."

"I didn't steal any letter," Ilse said. "I was just a translator."

"For criminals."

"I had to eat," Ilse said.

"Maybe, but the Pschorr shipping company seems to be the carrier for munitions shipped to Germany."

"Well, they haven't called me about it," Ilse said.

"Do the nationalists know that you're a Jewess?"

"Get to the point."

Mr. Benchley said, "We all know that you've read the letter that was stolen and are aware of its contents."

"I've already forgotten it."

"Really…?"

"Yes."

"You don't forget things like that," Mr. Benchley said. "And what did you tell the Major when he asked you about the letter?"

"You're making assumptions that I told him anything."

Mr. Benchley said, "A good journalist gets to the truth by doing that."

"Well, you're not getting to me."

"Maybe," Mr. Benchley said, "but should someone find out that you're a Jewess, well, there could be a bit of a problem."

"Are you threatening me?"

"I wouldn't do that," Mr. Benchley said.

"What are you doing then?"

"Not what you think."

Ilse got up and said, "Mr. Benchley, you're looking for information in a country with a phrasebook in your pocket. Learn the language and then I'll show you a few things."

Mr. Benchley said, "You take offence quickly."

"And you offend quickly."

She left the table and then the café.

17

The Lutheran

The footman led Major Coors through the hallway of Manfred Pschorr's Grunewald mansion, otherwise known as The Cottage because of its rolling thatched roof. The Major had expected to see creatures with tangled beards in ill-fitting black cloaks huddled around a Hebraic candelabra with branches reaching out like its people, all under the sound of pitched prayer, something that he had imagined when visiting Egon's hunting lodge across the lake. Instead, the Major was confronted with light and air. The Bauhaus influence everywhere. The library walls filled with books ranging from political science, economic theory, mathematics, history, the hard sciences, art, and in every language. The Major took note of the newest edition of *Die Dame* that was on the desk by the large window that faced the lake. The cover was of the Voodoo Child. Her hauntingly beautiful face and petulant blue eyes dismissed cheaper notions of beauty.

A tall blonde-haired man entered the room. He wore a bespoke suit that spoke of wealth and sophistication, sewn by tailors who worked for princes and understood the difference between formal and weekday pants, and that elegance was a mandate of power. The impact was immediate on the Major, who stood on his toes to gap their difference in height. Manfred Pschorr, a man used to giving orders and having them obeyed, told the Major to sit down. The Major obediently did and then felt ashamed for having submitted so easily, but—worse—the

Major wasn't offered any of the prized liquor on the rolling cart nor the tobacco in the humidor that was twice the size of Egon's.

Manfred Pschorr said, in the tone of a game warden collecting the day's hunt, "I just had word with Emil Hugenberg, and he suggested that your visit here wasn't his idea, even though he thought that it might behoove me to see you, which I find odd, since you have so little to offer me or anyone else."

The Major resented being treated as an inferior by someone whom he knew to be his complete inferior. "I find it odd that a Jew speaks as if he's a German."

Manfred Pschorr wondered what kind of idiot he had allowed into his home. "I'm a Lutheran. Not a Jew." He then pressed an electronic button beside his desk telephone that called for the footman.

The Major said, "And should I call myself a Jew, I am still a Prussian as you are still a Jew. But I'm not here to waste time. I want the release of the shipment."

"Shipment…?"

"The one in Hamburg."

"What shipment?"

"Herr Pschorr, I am here because your shipping company has no doubt been pressured by the illegitimate Jew government and its Jew ministers who have been clamping down on political groups that it disagrees with, which for any German is a crime of immense proportions."

Manfred Pschorr said. "Only a few in government are of the Hebrew persuasion."

"One is more than enough, and none is always an opportunity for more," the Major said, noticing a photo of this host in a Reichswehr officer's uniform wearing an Iron Cross First Class. "And I suppose now with the Dawes Plan, you Jews will be building more synagogues to scratch your beards."

"…Have you spoken with Mr. Dawes?"

"Herr Pschorr, he and the Jews are using the money to buy up the country, which is a crime gone unpunished."

"You have no proof of that, but then proof is not high up on your list, is it?"

"Dawes is controlled by them," the Major said.

"Name one of them."

"I'm not in the naming game."

"No, you're in the blaming game."

"I resent that."

"You resent everything."

"And for good reason," the Major said as he leaned toward his host. "Why are you Jews so obsessed with your religious laws and so deadly silent when the heart speaks?

"Major, the Jews are obsessed with their laws, because people like you have no heart."

"I won't play your silly little Jew game. To be a German is to be a nationalist. Anything less is a traitor, and a Jew is a traitor by his very nature. So, at least have the decency to release the shipment to Emil Hugenberg."

"Well, that's good to hear," Manfred Pschorr said.

"What's good to hear?"

"I'm a nationalist too."

"…How can *you* be a nationalist?"

"Everyone knows that I'm a nationalist."

"You're a Jew."

"I'm a Lutheran."

"You're a Jew," the Major said.

"I'm a German first, not a Lutheran, nor a Jew, nor anything else. And if you can't understand that, it's because you're a communist."

"I am *not* a communist, Herr Pschorr."

"That's what *you* say."

The Major stood up. "I'm a *nationalist* and nothing else. Don't put any labels on me."

"As far as I'm concerned, you're a whiny little communist."

"Who cares what *you* think?"

"Actually, Major, I don't know what the hell you are, other than a lunatic who walked in out of nowhere with his head up his ass."

The Major put both his hands on his host's desk and said, "I resent any Jew talking to me like that."

"You can resent it all you want."

"You'll apologize to me right now or we'll have a duel."

"Then you'll risk being made shorter than you already are."

The Major waved his finger at Manfred Pschorr and said, "I warn you, Jew, I want that shipment delivered as instructed or there will be trouble for all your people soon enough."

"Well, unless you have the original papers, nothing can be done about any shipment… By the way," Manfred Pschorr said, picking up *Die Dame* magazine. "I hear you're in love with this girl."

The Major said, "With your blood, you wouldn't have a chance with her."

"Well, then neither would you."

Confused, the Major said, "You're an idiot," and headed out the door. He went the wrong way and got thrown out by the footman.

18

Port of Hamburg

A derrick boom lowered a freight net into the cargo hatch of the *Pegasus*. Below deck, Captain Ellsworth Marsham stepped aside of the swinging net and said to Al Nachman, "I've got Germans on the quay eyeing this ship day and night."

"Have they tried to board the ship?"

"Not yet," Captain Ellsworth Marsham said, as he walked through the ship's cargo hold. He stopped at the wooden crates of munitions that bore the markings starting at 1917-SA-30 Lot 895. "This is what they want," he said, pointing to the long row of stacked crates bolted with nails and metal latches.

"When are you leaving port?"

"Within the week," Captain Ellsworth Marsham said, as the derrick boom aimed another loaded net down the hatch.

"We'll need around-the-clock guard on this ship."

"Already done," Captain Ellsworth Marsham said. "You mind telling me what the legal consequences would be if my sailors have to fire on German citizens, should it ever come to that?"

"This is a French registered ship," Al said. "Anyone on board is on French territory. The Germans pull any stunts, the French will love it. In the meantime, I'll be sending an associate of mine here to keep an eye on things. His name is Beau LaHood. He's a black American and I don't want anyone to treat him anything less than white."

"The only color that concerns me is when the sky turns gray."

"Good," Al said to the captain. "Now, I've got to catch the next train to Berlin and I should be there in just a few hours. You know where to reach me should anything happen."

"No doubt something will……."

Al headed to the Hamburg Hauptbanhof and boarded his train just as it was leaving. He found a compartment and was soon enough speaking German. One of the passengers, who sold Carl Tielsch shaving mugs, wanted Al to set him up with King C. Gillette safety razors for all of Germany. Al had to inform him that he wasn't in that line of work. The man undeterred, said, "But we could make a fortune."

Al told him, "Thanks, but I've had enough close shaves in my life," and parted ways.

19

Hotel Esplanade – Several Hours Later

"**I**s she there, please?" an unfamiliar male voice said, over the telephone, in a heavy German accent.

"Is who there?" Beau said, holding the candlestick telephone close to his mouth.

"Miss Prevette."

"Why do ya wanna know?"

The German said, "I'm an old friend."

"How old?"

"Very old."

"What's the name of her horse?"

"What…?"

"Her horse."

"Her *horse*?"

Beau said, "You don't know the name of her horse, you ain't an old friend."

"I forget the name."

"Ain't the only thing you forget," Beau said.

"What's your name?"

"Iffen you an old friend, you'd know my name."

"I forget."

"You remember why you called, or did you forget that too?"

"No. But you say to Miss Prevette to be outside from the Haus Vaterland by midnight in the Potsdamer Platz and alone and my gift to her will be given."

"Tell her yourself," Beau said, hanging up. There was a knock on the door. Beau took out his M1911 Colt .45 and held it at his side. "Who is it?"

"An old friend…"

Beau opened the door and laughed, "Seems a lot of old friends callin' this time of day." He put the gun away and shook hands with Al Nachman. "Good to see you. I got your wire. When did you get in?"

"Just in now from Hamburg. What's with the weapon?"

"There's been things goin' on ever since we got here."

"I've heard," Al said. "How are you?"

"So far, okay. Where're you stayin'?"

"Just down the hall," Al said. "They're sending up my trunk now. How's Miss Prevette?"

"Like tryin' to put a leash on a cat."

Al walked over to the other end of the room and stood by the window. He looked down into Potsdamer Platz, now the busiest hub of Europe with its bustle of cafés, shopping, and nightlife, and said, "Where is she?"

"Down at some big Berlin magazine for some interview."

"Interview…?"

"Seems the fashion folk is all thrilled an American socialite loves Berlin."

"How's your German?"

"Awful," Beau said, staring at his grammar book that was open on the writing table. "I can put some sentences together. I just can't do it the way the Germans do. Gonna be a while before I be fluent on any kinda level."

"You won't have to be fluent," Al said.

"I won't?"

"I speak German," Al said.

"Yeah, but why won't I have to be fluent?"

"I'll be giving you a hand."

"With what?"

"If you accept the offer," Al said.

"Accept what offer?"

"To join our firm."

"*Me…?*"

"Yeah, you."

"But I'm colored."

"I don't give a damn if you're pink. The work that you did in New York more than proved your capabilities and nerve."

"Well, Miss Shelby ain't gonna be too happy about that."

Al said, "You leave her to me." He then handed Beau a narrow box and told him to open it. Beau did, and to his surprise saw business cards with his name *Beau LaHood, Private Investigator*, printed at the bottom of each card opposite the firm's Clarksdale phone number, just the way it was on business cards that passengers had given him on the train to remember them by, and now people would have something to remember him by. He looked up from the beautiful cards and said, "I accept the offer."

"I was hoping you would."

They shook hands on it. Al said, "And don't ever again say, But I'm colored."

"I won't."

"Good, now have you seen Sarah Revenlöw Remley?"

"She went out last night and never come back."

"The name Magnus von Coors ring a bell?"

"Never stops ringin'."

"Why's that?"

"We all met him on the boat over," Beau said. "Was a Reichswehr army major in the war, and all that, and is now head of the DNF—I can't say the whole thing in German—but it seems him and Zola got some history."

"What kind?"

"I don't rightly know, though I doubt it's political. She don't care about that stuff," Beau said. "But the Major didn't like me one bit. Sneered at me every time I was in his company. He couldn't speak a word of English, but I didn't need to know German to know how much he despised me. Then I got a hold of some book to do with politics that shed a light on things."

"What book?"

"Book Miss Shelby bought. She wanted to know the fuss about some fool who claimed a lot of dumbass things."

"Such as…?"

Beau said, "That the German people got to strive by any means to clean the world up of people like me and that all methods was permissible such as lyin', betrayin', and killin' whether it be women and old folk, baby, or Slav, or whoever, and as weird as it sounds, it's right there in that book of his, iffen you don't believe me. Then he went on about Jews bein' a disease and Negroes and Slavs bein' subhuman and a whole a lot of other horseshit. Shelby read it to me in English."

"What was the name of the book?"

Beau took it off the dresser and handed it to Al who then flipped the pages over. Beau said, "You got any idea what's his problem?"

Al looked up from the book and said, "*He's* the problem," and tossed the book into the wastebasket where it landed upright with the Austrian's face on the cover and the title *Mein Kampf* beside it. Al said to Beau, "I've got to hurry out now and meet someone concerning a certain letter of release."

"You mean for them munitions."

Al stood at the door and said, "Seems you were working before you were even hired."

"Can't help it."

"Neither of us can," Al said. "That's why you're now part of the firm. Keep an eye on things till I get back."

20

Hickory Dickory Dock

Evelyn Cohen
50 Eldridge Street, 5A
Lower East Side, New York, USA

Dear Evelyn,
Everyone knows why Emily Fischbein didn't invite you to her terrific New Year's Eve party and that's because you fibbed that you'd be out of town. The fact that you were at some other party, around the corner on Ludlow Street, where a certain boy you have a crush on didn't come, is your own fault—he happened to have been at Emily's party and not only was he a good dancer, but he wore me flat out, and his brother borrowed a Tin Lizzy for the night, which makes me think that he stole it, but who cares? It had a rumble seat where you could neck in private and that's exactly what we did on our way down to that Chinatown speakeasy where we ate tons of chop suey and guzzled down rotten bathtub gin made in Shanghai, Brooklyn. But don't be disappointed; you've got good taste in boys.

Now about my father, the *big* liar. The things he said to you are not true! And since I wasn't at your sister Estelle's wedding to defend myself, he got away with saying whatever he could. So, let me make it clear, once and for all. I did *not* run away from home: I ran away from *him*. Oh, and that boy, Melvyn, that you such have a crush on? Tell him to stop writing me. I'm no longer interested. And good luck now that your sister is married, because the pressure will now be on you. If you should ever really need any advice, ask my father; he's *full* of it—pun intended. By the way, the reason that there's a foreign stamp on this letter is that some dumbbell I know forgot to mail it when he left New York.

Love,
Rachel

Ilse sealed the letter.

Oskar knocked on her bedroom door.

"Come in," she said, pointing to the bathroom. "Is there a water shortage?"

"I'm sorry, Mistress Ilse, but the city turned it off for several hours."

"What happened now?"

"There's a killer on the loose," Oskar said.

"What's that gotta do with the water?"

"I have no idea, Mistress Ilse, but the Major called and said that he's on his way for you to take him to the ball."

"What about my fan mail…?"

"I put the 62 bags of letters in the living room, but I've got a letter, here, that was hand delivered from that famous sexologist."

"You mean the one who has the same first name as the Major?"

"Yes, Mistress Ilse."

She crumpled it up and tossed it in the trash bin and then sat down at her makeup table and slicked her hair back with some Feinste Haar Pomade. "Oskar…"

"Yes, mistress?"

"Why do the men you detest always fall in love with you?"

"Oh, that's easy, Mistress Ilse."

Ilse closed her thin diaphanous robe and said, "Tell me. I'm *dying* to know."

"Men fall in love with you because they have eyes. Without them, they'd have to get to know you."

"Maybe, I don't want them to get to know me."

"Then as long as they can see you, I don't think you'll have to worry."

She dismissed Oskar and started writing her next letter.

Dear Uncle Barney,

I don't know where to begin, but since I'm sure the feds are stealing all the letters that I send you, I'm having a friend hand deliver this one to you. Now, what I'm telling you is secret, so don't ever say a word to anyone, but I'm stuck in crazy Berlin at the moment, and as you probably already know—unless you've been listening to all my father's hooey—the reason I came here was not because it's so cheap, but because *he's* so cheap. And when I got here, I got stuck at our cousins' lousy apartment over on Alexander Platz, and I really thought they'd be nice to me since they're on my mother's side but as soon as I unpacked, the four-flushers lined up to shake me down, and when they found out that I didn't have two-bits, things only got worse for me, especially since I can't get a regular job here because I'm not a citizen and don't have papers and all that, and soon enough I was living in the streets going hungry for days on end, without a roof over my head, and the holes in my shoes were only getting bigger by the hour. I must've passed Café Josty a million times hoping to snatch a cup of leftover coffee or a Linzer Tart someone had left on a table. And then, just as I was about to jump into the River Spree that twists around Berlin like a bad dream, I noticed a bunch of girls lined up on the Kurfürstendamm. I politely asked them what they were waiting for, but little did I know that they weren't brought up well. The flimflams all suspected that I was out for something that they themselves didn't yet have. So, I took a chance, because I had nothing to lose, except *more* weight, and got on the long line knowing that the gusher in charge would certainly look me over for whatever job he had to offer, even if I had no working papers as there are a lot of businesses here that pay under the table just like back home. Finally, we were allowed inside the joint, which I thought was a petting pantry, when I saw a sign that read: Heaven and Hell Cabaret. Guess what? We had to wait all over again, because making a girl wait is part of making her feel worthless so that when she's offered a job, she'll be willing to work for nothing. They did let us smoke, even though I couldn't even afford a cigarette, and those girls who were rich smoked and ate Limburger cheese, which only made me hungrier. Then the farshtunkenuh shicksas sneered at all the other girls in the line who had big noses, legs too short, backsides too big, toes too stubby, teeth too small, or gums too big. That's when I learned that all this waiting was for a dancing and acting audition, which should've been obvious, but then I'm a scholar not a schnorrer, and I couldn't care less about show business, and I have absolutely no interest in the acting department. I mean, how much brains do you need to think of lines that are already written for you? So, after what seemed to be ten years of waiting, a woman—dressed as a man—came out and said that she was the director of the cabaret's two stages. Her name is Siegfried, but once you get to know her you call her Ziggy, and yes, it's a phony name and everyone's got a phony name here, because a real name is so boring since you didn't give it to yourself. And so, when it was my turn to audition, she asked me what I could do in the dancing and acting department, and I told her not a damn thing. I mean I can do the Charleston and the Mud Bottom, and the Tango, but I'm no Oliver Twist. The only practice I've had kicking up my heels is kicking my tormentor back in the Lower East Side and now the Bronx. Well, as you can guess, Ziggy thought I was nuts and asked me what the heck was I doing auditioning and I told her that I needed a job and she told me that she was looking for a mesmerizing, beautiful girl, which I was, who had a mesmerizing powerful voice, which I didn't know I had, and a girl who knew how to use a whip, and so I fessed up and told her that what she was looking for was a carnival barker who had served time in Sing Sing. She said don't worry, all I had to do was recite *Hickory dickory dock. The mouse went up the clock* while flailing a whip. When I got done, she said that I had turned a nursery rhyme into a cosmic mystery —I have no idea what she meant, and I still don't. Now about the whip, I've never used one in my life, but all I had to do was think of all those teamsters and hansom cabbies whipping horses up and down Canal Street and the West Side docks when I was a kid, and that did the trick. But when I found out that I had to use it on people—I know what you're thinking, Barney, but look, a lot of horses are smarter than people so what's the difference who gets whipped? I got the job.

By the way, if you think they hate folks of the Hebrew persuasion back home, wait till you over get here. Never tell anyone here that you're of the persuasion unless you want people to instantly despise you. Lie to them. Make the sign of the cross. Even wear one. I bought a cheap one to throw around my neck in case of a pogrom. Luckily, with my blue eyes and shayneh punim, I've had no problem, because the only thing Jew haters think of when they see me is screwing me, which proves that a man can only be a racist when he's not horny. Then, for whatever reason, I became an overnight sensation in Berlin and I'm now on the cover of *Die Dame* magazine, which is like being on *Vanity Fair* or *Photoplay* back home, and in case you don't believe me, I'm stuffing a copy of the magazine inside this mail packet so you can see for yourself, but don't show it to my parents. You know how crazy my mother is wanting me to be a balaboostah.

So, that's it for now. Keep the lights on for me at your club and the Prohis away and write to me as soon as possible!

Aleh meyn liebe,
Your favorite niece,
Rachel

21

Unknown Man

Emil Hugenberg did not like the tone of the man on the telephone. "*Who* are you again?"

"I would tell you, Herr Hugenberg, but I don't see that it matters."

"And just how did you get my private number?"

"Herr Hugenberg, you were supposed to have had the shipment released by this morning."

"Who told you that nonsense?"

"You know who."

"No one told me anything."

"Herr Hugenberg, the copy of the letter of release is now in your hands, so it is very clear what has to be done."

"I would need to have the original document from New York, not some copy forwarded to me, and just who are you?"

"Are you trying to weasel out of things?"

"Don't you talk to me that way."

"Herr Hugenberg, we know that you are friends with that Jew shipper."

"What is your name or I'm hanging up?"

"Herr Hugenberg, all you have to do is call up your best Jew pal and get him to move his ass."

"He is not my friend."

"So, then, you know whom I'm talking about."

"Yes, but do you know what *you're* talking about?"

"Herr Hugenberg, you finally have the letter of release in hand. All you now have to do is to take it to Manfred Pschorr and get the shipment released."

"I'm sorry, but this is a fraudulent copy of the letter of release that was delivered to my house. Nothing can be done."

"And just how would you know that it's fraudulent, Herr Hugenberg?"

"Because anyone can spot a forgery, especially a cheap one like this."

"That's interesting," the unknown man said.

"*What's* interesting?"

"That you know what the original looks like, which means that you have the original, which means you've been hiding it from us all along."

"I haven't been hiding anything from anyone. Put von Coors on the phone."

"Who?"

"You know who. *Put* him on."

"Herr Hugenberg, if you do not leave the original document with your footman for us to pick up in the hour, we will assassinate you." The man hung up.

Al Nachman, sitting on the other side of the desk, handed Emil Hugenberg a folder. He opened it and read through the papers. He did not like what he saw.

Al said, "It would be a pity for you, if the press got a hold of these documents."

"I've just been threatened with assassination, and now you show me this," Emil Hugenberg said, looking up from a document. "And just how did Addison Prevette become the new owner of the Brush investment banking firm?"

"That's not the issue," Al said. "If anyone ever finds out that you, Thyssen, and von Remmele opened offshore accounts to hide money during inflation so that it wouldn't lose its value, you know what would happen to each one of you. Having said that, the funds for the munitions shipment have already been debited. And had Addison Prevette known about this deal, he would never have approved it. But then Brush, Bush, and Remley had purposely kept it from him."

"And I have no doubt that Prevette assassinated both Brush and Remley for that."

"Herr Hugenberg, that's what you Germans do. Those two men died in a boating accident as was reported in the newspapers."

"You believe that rubbish?"

"There's no reason not to," Al said.

"No one but an assassin would use explosives."

"There's a liquor war going on in America," Al said, "and people use whatever means, including explosives. Now, if you don't want the arms shipment, then I'll have it dumped overboard when the ship leaves port and enters international water, but the money is nonrefundable."

"You're stealing it, then."

"Not at all," Al said.

"You're bluffing."

Al got up and made his way to the door. "My business is done here."

"You're not going to leave me the original letter of release that we've already paid for?"

"Herr Hugenberg, I work for Addison Prevette, and he sees things differently than did Ellis Remley and Marbury Brush."

"That's because he's a thief."

"So are you, Herr Hugenberg; except that you're trying to steal a country......"

22

Miss Gorgeous

It was getting late, but Ilse needed to write one more letter before going to the tranny ball.

Effie Sonnabend
91 Rivington Street, 4C
Lower East Side, New York, USA

Dear Effie,
What on earth do you mean that you're lonely and nobody loves you and that you feel like it's the end of the world just because you got dumped for that scarecrow Hildie Meerapfel. Everyone in the world knows that you're as pretty and charming as she, but then boys are very good at falling love in with you and making you feel like you're the most special girl in the world and then dumping you after they've felt you up. What you need is practice in dumping *them*. And please stop telling everyone that I'm in Berlin. I'm really in Connecticut, but I have all my letters sent from Berlin so that no one knows where I am, and I may even invite you up for the weekend when things cool down. By the way, Connecticut is very nice, and they have some very nice trees, but if you say a word to anyone, I'll tell them your little secret about how you lost your virginity, which means good luck finding a husband.

Now, I've got to run. There's a big party down the road that a very nice bootlegger invited me to, and he smuggled hooch from Vermont, of all places, and I'd love to tell you who he is, but even the best of friends have mouths that move faster than their brains.

Love you so much, and don't kill yourself,
Rachel

Oskar knocked on the bedroom door.

"Come in," Ilse said, as she adjusted her men's tuxedo for the big ball tonight.

He entered and said, "You look magnificent, Mistress Ilse, and the monocle and top hat are just perfect."

"If this damn thing would only stay in," she said, trying to fit the eyeglass over her eye."

"The Major has arrived, Mistress Ilse, and he's waiting for you in the living room."

"Show him in. I want to see how he's dressed."

"Yes, Mistress Ilse."

Moments later, Oskar opened the door. Ilse had to lean over to get a better view of who was hiding outside. "Oskar, please tell Miss Gorgeous to enter."

The Major reluctantly made his entrance wearing a shimmering multi-colored drop waist dress with silver beads and a tiara on his head.

She said to him, "Fräulein Coors, you've never looked better in your life."

He said to her, "Just remember the speech that you're going to give at the party rally," the Major said. "It's part of the deal."

Ilse said, "I never made *any* deal, despite you having this weird notion that if you think of something that it's then automatically communicated to me." Oskar then helped her on with her black men's overcoat.

The Major walked over and said, "That was the deal. I dress up as a girl for the faggot ball and you speak at the rally."

"I never agreed to anything. You brought it up; I laughed. Now, let's go."

The Major stood before her and said, "You're going to keep your promise, Ilse. Everyone is expecting you at the rally. That's why I'm dressed up as a girl tonight."

"Magnus—you may even like it and do it more often."

"Ilse, you *made* me a promise, don't bullshit me."

"The only promises that I keep are the ones made to myself." She tried to move around the gender-cocktail and said, "And don't forget, *I'm* the man tonight, so you're going to have to do what I tell you and that means speaking to you the way you speak to a woman." Ilse headed out the bedroom door. On the street, several men passed by and whistled at the Major, which only made Ilse laugh harder as they got into a cab that took them to Würzburg Straße, saying, "They said they liked your ass."

"Fuck off."

Ilse reached into her dinner jacket for a smoke and waited for the Major to light it.

He said to her, "*You're* the man tonight."

She struck a match, but the Major couldn't stop squirming in his seat.

"What's the matter now, Fräulein Coors?"

"I'm freezing."

"I'm not," Ilse said.

"*I* am and down *here*."

"You're supposed to wear something underneath, Fräulein."

"I am, but—"

"What?"

"It's silky."

"What is?"

"The *hell* do you think?"

"I never get chilly down there," Ilse said, enjoying his discomfort.

"Well, that's because women's bodies are different. Their flesh naturally retains warmth for childbirth."

"You're sure about that?"

"Everyone knows that," the Major said.

"Well, for someone who's stabbed human beings to death, I find it amusing that chilled balls could be so annoying."

"*You* don't have any, so how would you know?"

"What I've got is better," Ilse said. "And who did your makeup?"

He touched his face. "…Something wrong?"

"It's magnificent for once."

"My ass it is, and I'm still waiting for an answer," the Major said.

"…Okay."

"Okay what?"

"Okay, I'll marry you," Ilse said.

"You *will*…?

"But under one condition."

"What?"

"That you wear women's clothes for the rest of your life."

The Major looked at her long and hard and said, "And what're *you* gonna wear…?

23

The Water Never Boils

Emil Hugenberg look troubled as he entered Egon von Remmele's library. Something had changed besides the evening light that shrouded the walls. He said to Egon, as he sat down, "I don't think you had those old weapons up there the last time I was here."

"They were there," Egon said, opening a bottle of schnapps.

Emil Hugenberg wasn't convinced as he fumbled with his chair. His coat was still on, despite the footman's disproval. "Do you know that the Major is going to a transvestite's ball tonight?"

Egon, pouring his guest a drink, said, "You're kidding me."

"No, it's some deal with Ilse so that she will give a speech at our next rally."

"Then the Major's smarter than I thought," Egon said.

"Dressing up in girl's clothes…?"

"My dear Emil, nothing is ridiculous after what happened in the war. We're still in a state of shock from its madness. So, people are questioning the old values. Some say that close to 50 million boys were killed in the war. Imagine losing 10 million a year, war or no war. Nothing is stranger than killing each other for no reason at all."

"Egon, you're sound like one of those Social Democrats."

"Emil, whether you're a Social Democrat or one of us, only a fool can justify losing 10 million boys a year, that is unless…"

"What?"

"Unless you tell your people that you've been stabbed in the back."

"But we were, Egon."

"We fucked up. But next time we won't. Next time there's a war, because there will be one, we'll fight it differently. Now, did you get the call from that American?"

"Call…?"

"Nachman," Egon said.

"Oh, him."

"And?"

"Well, he's not your typical slap on the back Yank."

"What did he say?"

"He's a spider," Emil Hugenberg said. "And now all my friends distrust me."

"Because of him?"

"Because of the Major…I don't know what happened, Egon."

"What do you mean?"

"He and I got along so well and now he's turned out to be a sniveling snake of the worst kind. There's something wrong with him— *you'll* be next."

"What about the American?"

"Look Egon, if anyone should find out about our offshore deposits—"

"*No* one will."

"Yes, but we'd all be thrown in jail, maybe worse, and you know what those sneaky shits will say—that when our country was starving and in need, we secretly hid our money, which isn't true, Egon. It isn't true. We were saving our funds so there'd be something left to invest in the Fatherland when things got better, though at the time I was sure that the end had come, but that's only normal and it's cruel when people gang up on you when they would have done the same thing."

"You're a worrier, Emil," Egon said, offering him a cigar.

"I'm a realist, and if I weren't so old, I'd challenge them all to a deadly duel, but at my age, the water never boils. I'm too smart for that.

Way too smart."

"I wouldn't worry," Egon said, offering his guest a light.

"I'm not worried the least," Emil Hugenberg said, leaving the cigar on the side table. "I'm just concerned."

"Of course, you are, but you need to remember that our allies are the judges in this country."

"…They are?"

Egon said, "They could have hung the Austrian. Instead, they sent him to Landsberg prison, and he was released in nine months, and that's because we've got the right people behind us."

"Who? Hitler?"

"The judges."

"But that was back in '23 when inflation was at its worst."

"So…?"

"Egon, you know as well as I that the economy is now coming along, and with the Dawes Plan people don't want any revolution; they want to spend money and have a good time."

"You're beginning to sound like those Social Democrat Jews."

"Not all of them are Jews, Egon; in fact, most of them aren't. But my first and only concern was and is the well-being of the Fatherland, but having it based on—"

"What…?"

"Egon, you have to see things strategically."

"What're you saying?"

"I've been thinking."

"You have?"

"It could be problematic."

"Thinking can be."

"Egon, I'm talking about race."

"As problematic?"

"I'm just saying."

"What are you saying?"

"I'm speaking in the strategic sense—the long term," Emil

Hugenberg said, "as it suits our needs."

"Whose needs?"

"Ours, Egon—if we just temporarily modify our stance now that the economy is brightening up—just a little bit. That's all. Just a little bit, until everything gets lousy again. Then we could really go after the Jews."

"I think you need another drink," Egon said.

"I haven't finished this one—and then you have to consider America's gross domestic product."

"I do…?"

"Yes, Egon, and despite America being a kennel hound of mixed races, its GDP is way off the charts, which just might give notion that our racial theories are just a little, well, you know, need some sprucing up."

"You think so…?"

"Well, with all that money flooding into the Fatherland, I mean, you don't want to be yelling fire where there isn't one."

"Emil…we Germans have won way more Nobel prizes for science than the Americans."

"A lot of them are Jews."

"Jews are on the Nobel committee, that's why."

"Nonsense, Egon; you know that's complete horseshit."

"They influence the committee, then."

"As much as they influence you," Emil Hugenberg said. "But what if, just what if, the Weimar Republic remains in power for the next 20 or *even* 50 years because of the Dawes Plan. I mean, think about that as a real possibility. Where would we be then if we continue to be so stubborn? A man has to be realistic, once a while."

"Of course, Emil, and that's why we can't sit around and wait, and I'm not talking about an all-out insurrection, that's been tried twice already. What we have to do is to put the heat on those in power, while remaining constitutionally minded citizens, and when the opportunity does arise, we'll be able to strike the iron when it's hot."

"Yes, but I just met up with some Americans, who were all excited about doing business here and spending a lot of money. Now, would you have wanted me to have told them that America is a nation of half breeds? Of course not, so I kept my mouth shut and for good reason, because of the investments that are at stake, and sometimes that's more important than our ideals, of course only sometimes."

"Emil, you cannot live life without making enemies and without ideals. A man who doesn't have enemies doesn't have character. A man who has no ideals is a piece of shit."

"I did *not* say to give up our ideals, Egon, just temporarily suspend them for the moment, a very short time until things get bad again."

"What about the shipment?"

"The what…?"

"The shipment. What about it, Emil?"

"That sniveling spider American is in the way. Now, *I'm* not suggesting anything, but if he could somehow disappear, it certainly wouldn't be to our disadvantage."

"Emil, should that American be stupid enough to do what he's inferred, concerning our finances, all we have to do is tell the world that it was Jewish money and not ours that had been deposited overseas. And you know that to be true, anyway."

"True…?"

"You know what I mean, Emil."

Well, maybe, yes, but what if that doesn't work? I mean you have to think of those things, Egon. You can't always blame it on the Jews."

"Oh, you *wanna* bet…?"

Emil shrugged it off for whatever it was worth. Egon said, "Have you spoken to the shipper?"

"The shipper…?"

"That Jew shipper. Your friend Pschorr—Manfred Pschorr about releasing the shipment."

"Egon…"

"What did he say?"

"Your wife is half Jewish."

"*He* said that?"

"I'm saying it."

"She's no longer a Jewess," Egon said.

"And just how did you accomplish that?"

"Emil…There are exceptions to everything in life, otherwise life would come to a standstill."

"What's the exception?"

"Once an exception is made it is no longer an exception, but Manfred Pschorr is *no* exception."

"Hitler would not agree with your theory of exceptions."

"Oh, in fact, he would," Egon said, pouring himself a little more whiskey, now. "You see, Emil Maurice, his confidant, is part Jew and not only did he go to Landsberg prison with Hitler for their insurrection against the Fatherland, but he's also one of two founding members of the SS. Hitler is registered as SS member number 1, Maurice number 2. So according to Hitler, if Maurice is not a Jew, then my wife is not one. So don't create a racial problem when there isn't one."

"What about your children?"

"What about them?"

"Egon…."

"What?"

"I hear that they're being called dirty Jews by certain people who are against us."

"Emil, I know all about that and those idiots will be seen to when we come into power. Now what about the letter of release?"

"I just told you that that American Jew spider is in our way, and he insists that New York will not return our money."

"Then we'll have to deal with him"

"I must warn you, Egon."

"What?"

"Nachman is the kind of man who casts more than one shadow."

"…What do you mean?"

"You think he's here, then he's there."

"I think you've had too much to drink, Emil."

"Not at all," Emil Hugenberg said, showing him his full glass. "And he's smart. Fearless. Danger is like candy to him."

"Too bad he's not on our side, but then…."

"What?"

"He's a Jew."

"Yes, Egon, but—"

"What?"

"As you say, there *are* exceptions……."

24

Opium

Zola's hazy eyes drifted to the Chinese man wearing a blue silk embroidered phoenix peony court gown. He was backlit by the little things that he knew. Zola found his face, but not his person. He said to her, in German, holding out a pipe, "More?" Zola, buck naked, said, "My dress. Where is it?" He went across the room where several women and a man were on mats staring into nowhere, their opium pipes already cold. He pulled her dress out from under them and gave it back to Zola. She slipped it on and then, on all fours, searched for her purse that had the ticket to the tranny ball. She found it empty.

25

The Ball

Shelby wore black tie, hair slicked back with Dapper Dan Pomade brought from home. With a tranny in arms, she danced over to Ilse and the Major and said to him, "You look gorgeous in that little tiara." The Major, eyes always bigger than his face, stuck out his tongue.

"And where's your cousin?" he said.

"I have no idea."

"Is she with a client?"

Shelby ignored him and said to Ilse, in English, "Let's dance."

"My pleasure," Ilse said, letting go of the Major. The tranny now in his arms, Ilse in Shelby's, as they went deeper into the dance floor and did the Black Bottom, the Shimmy, the Texas Tommy, the Grizzly Bear all in step and fired up. The music stopped, but not the drums as they savagely pounded on. Everyone fell into a line and did *Le Danse Sauvage*: Josephine Baker's hip throbbing jungle waltz with its corkscrew rattle and banana tussle that had taken over Paris and now Berlin. The line snaked through the hall and shimmied to the beat, and when it passed the champagne bar, Ilse and Shelby jumped out of line, eyes locked into each other, Shelby saying, "How did you get the Major to wear a dress?"

"No one likes to dress up more than a nationalist," Ilse laughed, giving her more powder.

Shelby feeling eight miles high, said," I'm really gone tonight."

"This is Berlin. You leave yourself at the door."

"Yeah, but which door?" Shelby said, her eyes now fixed on Ilse's. "I heard that you're leaving town and going to Bavaria."

"Your cousin talks too much."

Shelby said, "I love her, but she's crazy."

"The hell does she sees in the Major anyway? He's a total fuck."

"Never try to understand what people see in each other," Shelby said, "because over time they can't see it either…What's Fastnacht?"

Ilse said, "It's when the spirits summon the world and strange things happen."

"You don't believe that?"

Ilse into leaned Shelby and felt the heat in her eyes. "It's strange how fast we've become friends."

Shelby said, "I knew we would as soon as I walked into your dressing room, despite the situation."

Ilse said, "I didn't" and kissed her.

26

The Next War

Earlier that evening.

Police Inspector Max Degler rowed across the Grunewaldsee lake toward Egon von Remmele's mansion lodge. When he was close enough, he reached for his field glasses and panned the shoreline. A man with a little mustache stood outside the lodge's portico doing all the talking. Egon listened while his wife came down the lawn with a plate of powdery chocolate creampuffs for the Austrian's journey back to Bavaria. He bowed and thanked her for fetching his favorite food and then bade everyone goodbye. He was driven off in his 1923 Mercedes 11/40.

Inspector Degler rowed back to the other side of the lake where the rental boats were stored and left it with the attendant who had been called out of hibernation. The inspector got into his 1924 Kenter 5/18 and drove around the lake until he reached the long driveway of the Remmele hunting lodge. The hall porter received the inspector and escorted him down a long hallway to the huge library. Another ten minutes passed before the lodge master, as Egon liked to be called, slipped through the secret panel, and said with irritation, "What brings you here?"

The inspector said, "Why the hidden door?"

"When this house was built there was a need for such things. Now it is used by everyone."

Inspector Degler accepted the answer and walked over to the oversized window that faced the Grunewaldsee and observed not only Manfred Pschorr's stately cottage on the other side, but a flock of martens flying over in single file in the moonlight. "How many species of birds call this area home?"

Egon showed impatience and said, "I have no idea."

"I find it odd that people don't know their neighbors."

"I know my neighbors," Egon said.

"Yes, but people only know whom they wish to know. In the animal kingdom, the slightest ruffle, the snapping of a twig, a cooing in the treetop, a sudden splash, will signal danger or the next meal."

"You've come all the way here to tell me that?"

"Herr von Remmele, we are always in danger of something, but human nature ignores that which doesn't pleasure the moment, despite any imminent threat."

"…You're saying I'm in danger?"

The inspector turned away and took in the immense library with all its ancient weapons for hacking heads and limbs that occupied one wall. "Herr Remmele, I know that you miss the old days of empire when war seemed easy, and victory was a five-step waltz."

"I never said war was easy."

Inspector Degler said, "Neither is peace, as we are now forced to pay reparations for four years of bloody warfare in return for what the French had to pay after two weeks of defeat back in 1870."

"The French started that war, inspector."

"Bismarck instigated it, to put it lightly."

"One has to take leadership and Bismarck did exactly that," Egon said, "and that's what's missing today."

"Maybe, though you'll get nowhere living in the old world — the new one has already shown us that it has its own rules, which only a fool would ignore by indulging in self-pity and stabbed-in-the-back nonsense to assuage what is basically a self-inflicted wound. Nevertheless, Germany was and still is a great country, but it wasn't created by crybabies who denied reality. That's something your ancestors well understood when they built those steel mills in the Ruhr. It took men of steel to make steel. The Austrian has never built a thing. He's a man of talk who only makes talk. And if you follow him, you'll soon be talking to yourself."

"Maybe, Inspector Degler, but you do not send millions of men to die on the battlefield unless you plan to win or, for that matter, lose decisively."

"Herr Remmele, you forget that on the home front women and children were eating their shoelaces as three million American soldiers, pink in flesh and overfed, flooded France, while the English navy starved us with their iron clad blockade. If you call that getting stabbed in the back, then you were facing the wrong way."

"The next war will resolve that."

Inspector Degler put on his hat and went to the door. "Well, I'm here to make sure that there isn't one. So, don't even think about going near that ship in Hamburg."

"Is that why you came?"

"And it's why I'm leaving......"

27

The Keys

Daybreak found the Major climbing up the stairway to Ilse's apartment. The maintenance man quarreled with the Major's feminine attire, but when he saw money, he opened the door. Once inside, the Major went to straight Ilse's bedroom and turned on the lights. "*Get out* of here," Ilse yelled, holding the bedsheet over herself. The Major ripped it off. "The hell are you doing with her?" meaning Shelby.

"What I would do with a man, just differently." Ilse reached for her shirt that was on the floor. The Major kicked it away."

Ilse said, "*Get* the hell out of my apartment."

"I should've known," the Major said.

"There's a lot of things you've should've known."

"You make me sick."

"I only make *you* sick," Ilse said, "but you make *everyone else* sick."

"Get your ass out of bed and get my clothing from Ziggy's apartment."

"Get it yourself."

"It's *daylight*," the Major said. "People will see me."

"They didn't see you on the way here?"

"You live closer."

"Not any closer than Ziggy," Ilse said, getting out of bed with her hand out. "Gimme the damn keys."

The Major took them out of his purse and gave them to her.

Ilse said, "I'm gonna get your clothing, so you'll get the hell outta of here."

Shelby reached for her shirt, but the Major said, "You're not going anywhere until she gets back......"

28

The Red Castle

7:00 a.m.
Inspector Degler entered the palatial lobby of the Red Castle police headquarters that squatted over Alexander Straße. It had gotten its nickname from the red bricks and cupola towers that dominated the side corners and midblock entranceway. Its immense posture suggested that its source of power was absolute, something that wasn't lost on certain people. A clerk from the political office, who had been waiting in the huge lobby, ran over and handed the inspector a folder and said, "Sir, the translation of her newest letter is inside with all the others."

Inspector Degler took the folder to his private office and read the translation. He then tried to read the original, despite his poor English.

Ida Krepsig
44 Kesselstraße Berlin

Dear Ida,
I'm beyond grief concerning your brother. Misery's envy cuts you down with no reason other than that you might have been happy for one damn second but take pleasure that my fury against these cold-blooded clowns shall not dissipate once pen

is dropped. But first, kiss his grave for me, I loved him so. Every moment gone is a tear from me.

Love,
Ilse

Inspector Degler put the letter aside and reached into his briefcase for the most recent issue of *Die Dame* magazine that had the Voodoo Child's highly coded face on the cover. Her intelligence and sensuality were just one piece of the puzzle that had gripped Berlin. He flipped through the photos of the Heaven and Hell Cabaret and of the private dinner parties that Ilse had attended with luminaries who came from all over Europe to meet the teenager. He looked up from the magazine. There she was. "…What are you doing here so early?"

Ilse grabbed her letters and said, "You make me sick."

"You were supposed to be here later."

"You have a lot of damn nerve arresting *me* for stealing letters."

"They were intercepted, *not* stolen."

"Bullshit."

"When we make an appointment in Germany, unlike in your country, you arrive at the designated hour and on time."

Ilse said, "There was nothing in your message that said that I couldn't come earlier, and since I was on my way to get something, I thought I'd save time and stop by, and it's a *good* thing I did, because I'm now going to the robbery division to get you arrested for mail theft."

"Don't waste your time."

"It's my time to waste," Ilse said.

"Go ahead, but I'm running a criminal investigation concerning the fate of our democratic republic. The possibility of it failing is what should make you sick."

"I suppose my letters are a threat to its survival," Ilse said.

"I had to read them to find that out, but then you can go back to jail if you'd prefer."

"For sending letters to friends?"

"For not having left the country as ordered by the court," Inspector Degler said. "And I could put you away for five years, right now."

"I had no money to leave then."

"You do now," Inspector Degler said.

"Yeah, and I can go to the editrix of *Die Dame* and have her run a story about you stealing my mail."

"Well, if you do," Inspector Degler said, "don't forget to tell her that Ilse Dietrich is really the Jewess Rachel Pschorr who is the cousin of Manfred Pschorr, which should interest a lot of very excitable people."

"*Get* to the point."

"I want that letter of release," the inspector said.

"You had it when you arrested me."

"Yes, but we didn't know that it was connected to munitions then; it was seen as just another robbery—but you're the one who translated it."

"It was just some document about a shipment," Ilse said.

"For whom was it consigned?"

"I don't remember," Ilse said.

"Was the name Hugenberg, von Remmele, or von Coors in it?"

"It was a revised letter," Ilse said.

"What do you mean revised?"

"On the third page there was a cross-out of the original recipient," she said, "and them something about a secondary letter for the release to be executed."

"And who has this secondary letter?"

"I have no idea. Go to New York and find out."

Inspector Degler reached into his drawer and pulled out a court document that he pushed across his desk. "Read it...Then look behind you."

She read it and then saw a man with little room in his eyes crowding the doorway.

Inspector Degler said, "You're going to get the secondary letter of release from Fräulein Prevette and bring it to me as soon as possible."

"You're sure she has it?"

"At the moment, I don't know who has what," the inspector said. "I'm just asking you to help the fate of the republic, if it isn't too much trouble, and since Ida Krepsig's brother was beaten to death by Nazi thugs, it should only behoove you more to help your adopted country, as you speak German like a native."

"And what if Fräulein Prevette doesn't have it?"

The inspector said, "Then you're going to find out who does."

"Or what…?"

"Or you're going back to jail for five years as stipulated by law. Now, unless you like lice crawling in your underwear and food, I suggest that you get that letter."

Ilse said, "You forget that someone with power got me out of jail and will do it again."

"*I* got you out of jail."

"*You* did?"

"You didn't even know von Coors then," the inspector said.

"Yeah, but Klopp was hired by the Deutsche Nationale Freiheitspartei, and so the Major had to know who I was. He even said so."

"He's a liar," the inspector said. "We let you and Klopp out of jail to keep an eye on you two—by the way, how's Oskar?"

"Oskar…?"

"Your servant."

"He's fine."

"He's a detective in our unit."

"He's also a panty sniffer."

Inspector Degler shrugged his shoulders. "No one's perfect."

"What about the man in the Homburg, who's been hanging outside my apartment?"

"I have no idea who he is."

"You're lying," Ilse said.

"Fräulein, unless he's Oskar, I wouldn't know."

The telephone rang. Inspector Degler took the call. A moment later he looked up and said, "…It seems your friend Fräulein Prevette has just been kidnapped."

"Are you sure of that?"

Inspector Degler said, "Our man at her hotel just informed me that a note has been left for her servant concerning this."

"When did this happen?"

"You mean when was she kidnapped?"

"Yeah."

"That I don't know," Inspector Degler said, "but generally kidnappers wait until the victim is well hidden, before contacting anyone."

"Then it couldn't have happened in the past few hours."

"Most probably not."

"Good," Ilse said, heading out the door.

"Where are you going, young lady?"

"You want that letter of release?"

"Yes."

"Steal one more letter of mine and you're not getting it…"

29

Markelstraße 27

As soon as Ilse left the Red Castle, she called home from a street telephone. The Major picked up. She said to him, "Put Shelby on the phone."

"Where the hell are you?"

"Put her on the phone."

"You're telling me what to do?"

"Magnus—you *want* your clothes?"

"She's in the bathtub."

"*Put* her on the phone."

"The sooner you get me my clothes, the sooner you two can get back to screwing."

"Why did you kidnap her?"

"How could I have kidnapped her, if she's in the bathtub?"

"Very easily," Ilse said.

"I suppose you think I knew you two would be fucking here?"

"The police know about the kidnapping, so stop the bullshit."

"The police are playing with your head to get the letter of release. But your lover is right over there in the bathtub and she's not getting any further than that," the Major said. "Now get my clothing."

"I may get more than that……"

Ziggy's apartment was on Markelstraße 27. Ilse knew it well as she had lived there when Ziggy had first hired her. The Major lived there too, and he would always wander into the living room where Ilse slept on the couch, and go on about politics and war, especially his fondness for the trenches and the rats that tunneled into the stomachs of dead boys for their tasty livers, spleens, and hearts—his way of impressing her. He would go on about how the Fatherland had been stabbed in the back and she would always remind him, "You lost the war, because you fucked up." The Major, not to be outdone by a girl, took the manly way to reason and told her that girls didn't know anything about war, and then went on about how he had slit the softest part of an English boy's belly before yanking a sawback bayonet up through his ribcage to finish him off. The Major even showed her how it was done with a couch pillow, saying that the intense pleasure of killing was in surviving the horror, not in denying it, although she already knew what his real pleasure was. He even offered her the bayonet as a token of his affection as he was now convinced that she had been taken in by his manliness. She took it, but not out of love.

Ilse went into the Major's cramped bedroom. It was full of junk from the war as well as his party posters that he had tacked on the walls. One of them, from the crazy days of inflation, depicted a crowd of hapless souls etched in misery. Written across the top in bold words were: **YOU WERE SOLD OUT,** and at the bottom: **KNOW WHO YOUR FRIENDS ARE — VON COORS**. Then there were the racial posters of the Nordic man perfectly balanced in form and intention; his only fault was that he wasn't real.

Ilse having had enough of the Major's private museum, stuffed whatever clothes of his that she could find into a bag and hurried down the stairway only to run into the man with the Homburg in the lobby. He chased her down the street as madly as he could.

30

The Joy of Home

The Major was stretched out on Ilse's living room couch, his dress bunched up, and on the telephone with one of his trusted party men, Otto Zumbach.

"…Are you *sure* of this?"

Otto Zumbach said, "I'm not only sure of it, but the lie comes straight from Hitler's cripple and he's on his way over here to take over the NSDAP office to make a bigger footprint in Berlin, and before he left Munich, he said that the DNF is nothing but a Jew party."

"What else did the cripple say?"

Otto Zumbach said, "That he's going to kick us out of Berlin."

"Then he's gonna have his other leg to worry about."

Otto Zumbach said, "Yeah, but could there be any truth to what the cripple is saying about Ilse?"

"What did he say?"

"That she's a Jewess."

"I'll kill him for that."

"He's also saying that you're a Jew lover and that they're financing our party."

The Major said, "Then we're going to say the same thing about the Nazis."

"Well, if you want to tell everyone that Hitler is a Jew, fine with me, because for all we know, he might really be one. But he and his cripple are trying to destroy Ilse's credibility, before she gives her speech at our rally."

The Major said, "So, that's why Hitler was at von Remmele's dinner parties, to meet her, and it seems that he was impressed enough to put the cripple on her."

"Well, it was a smart move on their part, and I think von Remmele was behind all of it."

The Major said, "We'll deal with him soon enough."

"Yeah, but he's our source of money."

"He's also become the source of all our problems. What about the other girl?"

"She fits the description," Otto Zumbach said. "Our men heard an American accent, and she had the same haircut, so you can't blame them."

"Excuses add up to nothing. Accomplishments add up to everything."

Otto Zumbach said, "We'll get the other girl, don't worry. But rumor now is spreading that Manfred Pschorr is Ilse's uncle, if you can believe that one."

"More bullshit," said the Major.

"They're saying her real name is Rachel Pschorr."

"And mine is Santa Claus."

"But what if it's true?"

"It's not."

"What if it *becomes* true…?"

The Major said, "We'll kill him."

"Who?"

"The cripple."

The door of the apartment opened.

The Major lowered the phone from his ear.

Ilse went straight to her bedroom then back to the living room and tossed the Major's clothing on the couch. "Get off my phone."

The Major whispered to Otto Zumbach, "Get moving, now." He hung up and got off the couch. "Why the hell are you so late?"

"*Someone* is missing," Ilse said.

"Who?"

"You know who," Ilse said.

"No one is missing, and why is it when a man tries to be nice to you, you're always a pain in the ass?"

"*Get* dressed."

The Major took his clothing and said, "Let me remind the most fascinating girl in all of Europe that she was recently living in the gutter whoring herself."

"I never whored," Ilse said.

"Oh, I forgot; you're Mary Pickford, the princess of American movie crap."

"You're sick, Magnus. Now get dressed and get out."

"Darling Ilse, you seem to be upset once again. Is there something troubling you?"

"You're goddamn right there is. Where's Shelby?"

"In the bathtub."

"No, she isn't." Ilse said.

The Major went to look for himself. Then he searched the rest of the apartment and said, "A girl who tries to be clever is very dangerous."

"The Austrian said that at von Remmele's dinner party the other night, so think up your own crap."

"He wasn't all that wrong," the Major said, tucking in his shirt and buttoning his pants.

"Why did you kidnap her? To get the letter of release?"

"Didn't you see the bubble bath in the tub?"

"Yeah, but I didn't see her," Ilse said.

"Do you really think that I could arrange a kidnapping *and* a bubble bath that quickly?"

"You had more than an hour to do so."

"*Waiting* for you," the Major said.

"*Where* is she?

The Major tucked in his shirt and said, "I have no idea."

"You kidnapped her."

"While wearing a dress?"

"That wouldn't be beneath you," Ilse said.

The Major combed his hair and straightened out his tie in the cabinet glass reflection.

"Where is she, Magnus?"

"I have no idea. But at the moment, my real concern is *you*."

"What did you do with her?"

The Major said, "I'll find her, alright. You can be sure of that."

"You damn well better."

"Ilse, I understand your romantic anxiety."

"You understand nothing."

The Major said, "A woman's greatest fear is to be ignored."

"What're you talking about?"

"The mind of a woman, but then you're not listening."

"Why would I want to listen to you?"

"Because," the Major said, "I have done nothing but observe women all my life and undesirability horrifies them like nothing else, and for that alone, a woman spends all her time buying silly clothing, applying vast amounts of useless cream to her face just so that someone might look at her and think that she still smells as fresh as a daisy when she really stinks like a—I won't even say it."

"That's *your* greatest fear."

The Major turned away from his reflection in the cabinet window and said, "Ilse, why is it when you try to be funny, I never laugh?"

"That's something you should look into."

"I already have," the Major said, "but then it's hard to be amused by a girl who resorts to hysteria when she doesn't get her way."

"*What* happened to Shelby?"

"Hand me my suit jacket." Ilse did. He slipped it on and said, "By the way, I went through you all your clothing, all your pretty shoes and pretty dresses and pretty hats and pretty things that a girl requires before spreading her legs. I won't have that when we get married."

"You're sick."

"Then we're all sick," the Major said, "but one thing has been certain since the moment of creation."

"You weren't there, so how do you know?"

"I didn't have to be there to know that a woman's real purpose in life is to be the joy of home, not be a miserable bitch who fucks women."

"You seem to forget that the Nazi Brown Shirts are all faggots who take it up the ass."

"…I'll concede that," the Major said, combing his hair again in the cabinet window reflection.

"The police know that you kidnapped Shelby."

"I suppose they called you up for your expert advice on pussy criminology."

"They must think so," Ilse said. "I was just at the Red Castle."

The Major turned away from the cabinet window and stared at her, "Doing *what*?"

"I…I was picked up on my way out. That's why I was late. And they know about the message left at her hotel and the ransom note—you won't get away with this."

"Ilse darling, when I walked in here this morning, I had no idea that Fräulein Prevette was here, and you know that. So, this nonsense about me kidnapping her is something the police invented so that you would get them the letter of release, and since you and that nasty Fräulein Prevette have become such big hands-in-your-panties buddies, you should get it for *me*, although now it may not even be necessary."

"And just what makes you think the police wanted *me* to get it?"

"Ilse, I have my sources. Now, let's get down to business." He picked up his hat and shaped the crown. "I want you to stay home all day," the Major said.

"Just who are you to order me around?"

"Ilse darling, it's your day off. I don't want you tired for tonight."

"Tonight…?"

"We have a date."

"Since when?"

"Since now," the Major said, taking her by the arm.

"I already have a date and *let go* of me."

"You're dating *me*, Ilse, *not* a girl."

"Magnus. You and I hate each other. Why would you ever think that we could be dating?"

"Why would I think not?"

"You're sick, Magnus. You *really* need help."

"Actually, I'm the healthiest man on the planet. My doctor said that I'll live to 210." The Major took Ilse down the hallway. "I'm going to have to lock you in your bedroom until I get back tonight."

"*Let go of me.*"

"You've got a speech to give, and you need to be fresh as a daisy. Tonight, we'll go over the finer points of it."

She tried kicking him away.

The Major said, as they entered her bedroom, "But, first, we have to clear up a nasty little rumor that's been going around."

"I can only imagine."

"People are telling me that your real name is Rachel Pschorr."

"My name is Ilse. I live on the second floor—and *let* go of me."

"Then who is Rachel Pschorr?"

"I have no idea."

"Ilse," the Major said, now in her face, "we may fight and call each other names, but lovers fight all the time and not because they hate each other, but because they share the same displeasure in a world they're forced to live in. But these insidious lies that have been spreading around concerning your blood have become most troubling. So, I'm going to ask you out of love and not hate, and this time you're going to tell me the truth, even though I know what it has to be."

"Tell you *what?*"

"Are you impure?"

"…What do you mean by impure?"

"It's very simple. Are you Aryan or are you vermin?"

"I'm neither."

"You're either one or the other, Ilse. You don't need an advanced degree in physics to understand that."

"I'm neither."

"Ilse dear, you must answer the question."

"What do you want me to say, Magnus? Tell me and I'll say it."

"I want you to tell me that you're not a fucking Yid."

"I'm as Jewish as Jesus."

"You're trying to be funny again," said the Major.

"Then why aren't you laughing?"

"Say something in Jew talk and maybe I will."

"You don't know how to laugh."

"Ilse, darling, this gossip about you being a Yid has to stop once and for all, and since I'm a genius, I shall use the counterintuitive method."

"And just what the hell is that?"

The Major said, "I have the amazing ability to see through all lies. Now, *are* you a fucking Yid?

"…You *really* want to know?"

"*Yes.*"

Rachel sang the Ha'tikvah in the same eerie tone that she had sung the German national anthem at the Heaven and Hell Cabaret…then things got ugly.

Shelby was on the line with Beau in a public telephone several blocks away. He was telling her, "Give me Ilse's address and we'll meet up outside her building and take it from there."

She gave Beau the address and telephone number and said, "How long will it take for you to get here?"

"Just hurry back to the buildin' and wait outside for me, but iffen you should see Ilse, stop her from goin' upstairs. That's all you gotta do for now……"

Shelby hung up and crossed Barbarossa Platz to Franken Straße and saw the Major leaving Ilse's building. His hair was mussed, suit rumpled, eyes distant. The sweat on his face, part grime, part crime.

Shelby quickly stepped into a nearby building and waited for him to go by. Then she hurried down the street and went up the two flights of stairs to Ilse's apartment and knocked hard on her door. She waited a moment, despite the Peeping Tom down the hall, and opened it. She then searched the apartment and found Ilse on her bedroom floor, face down in blood.

Shelby had never made coffee, let alone cooked anything in her life and it showed when she poured what looked like dirty water into Ilse's cup. "You sure nothing's broken?"

"You sure this is coffee?" Ilse said, as she tried to find a position on the sofa where she could lean without any pain.

"We should call a doctor. Your face is swollen."

"It's a little early to find one."

"We could try."

"Look, I'm not even supposed to be in the country, so I'm not going to any hospital or doctor where they ask you a ton of questions." Ilse's hand shook as she put down the lousy coffee. "The Major thought that I was dead. That's why he ran away."

"He looked like someone was after him."

"I was," Ilse said.

"*You* were?"

"I was floating."

"What…?"

Ilse sat up and waved her arms.

Shelby said, "It was just the shock of what that son of a bitch did to you."

"It was *because* of what he did," Rachel said, pointing toward the ceiling. "And I was up there looking down at myself."

"Up where?"

"*There*," Ilse said, pointing straight up.

"You were upstairs?"

"No."

"You just pointed there," Shelby said.

"Yeah, but I wasn't upstairs."

"Then, where were you?"

"I was dead."

"You were *what?*"

"That's what they call it," Ilse said.

"Maybe it's the coffee I made," Shelby said.

"No, and I was zooming away at this incredible speed."

"…What're you talking about?"

"I was out there," Ilse said, pointing anywhere. "A zillion miles a second and then—I saw my late grandfather."

"Where?"

"*There*, and he wasn't all that happy to see me."

"You mean upstairs?"

"*No.* Another dimension, one of many others."

"Look," Shelby said, "you were out of it for the moment. Things happen."

"I certainly was out of it," Rachel said, sitting taller, hands steadier. "My grandfather left this world five years ago, but I saw him as clear as day."

"You were dreaming. That's all."

"You have to be asleep to dream," Ilse said.

"You were daydreaming."

"No. He said to me, 'What're *you* doing here?' as if I had done something wrong, and I said to him, 'I'm in such pain, please help me,' but there was nothing that he could do and I pleaded with him and then he walked through me or became part of me; I can't explain it, but that's what happened."

"You were under stress, that's all," Shelby said.

"No, this was different."

"Maybe you need something to eat."

"I don't want anything to eat," Ilse said.

"Maybe some good coffee?"

"I don't want that either," Ilse said.

"Well, how do you talk to someone who's dead?"

"No one is dead."

"…What're you talking about?"

"Look," Ilse said, "death is just a name we apply to something that scares the hell out of us, something that we don't understand. It's that steep ledge that we're always looking over and culturally we've made sure that it's always there beside us."

"How can you not fear death?"

"I just told you," Ilse said.

"Well, I must've missed it."

Ilse said, "Fear of death is dismissed by deconstructing its implied meaning, which is based only on fear and not real experience; in other words, the false experience of assuming that the very stillness of body, as seen by our eyes, implies personal annihilation."

"But you have to be dead to experience that."

"Dead as *you* define it," Ilse said, "but I not as I experienced it."

"But you're alive."

"You're *always* alive," Ilse said. "That's the joke that no one gets."

"…You're telling me there's no such thing as death?"

Ilse said, "It exists only as it is defined, not as it is experienced."

"Didn't you just do that? Define it?"

"No, I experienced it and described it."

Shelby said, "Well, I don't want to have to die to experience it."

"You have no choice. One day you will."

"Well, I'm not looking forward to it. Now, what about your grandfather?"

"I wanted him tell me the meaning of life," Ilse said. "Why all the madness and brutality? And he said to me, 'I can't tell you,' and I said, 'You have to tell me. I'm going nuts,' and he said, 'If I do, *they* will take you out of there.'"

"*They*…?"

"Yeah, *they*," Ilse said.

"Who are *they?*"

"The puppet masters, controllers, whoever. But any label is insufficient as all labels are categories exclusive to certain limited sources of information that invariably lead to a dead end when invalidated by newer sources."

Shelby said, "That can mean you as well."

"But it doesn't mean that I'm wrong."

"…What did you mean *there?*"

"*Here.*" Ilse said. "And then some old lady was there."

"Who…?"

"She had eyes so dark with visions tangled in different times that you could see the future in its finest thread. And then she told me that I'm one of the three ancient Norns and somehow, I don't know how, I knew what she meant—again, she was speaking in categories or types, but I fully understood it to mean the nature of time as it really is and not how we imagine or describe it."

"What about the future?"

"Forget the future; it's already set," Ilse said.

"How can it be set?"

"In that there is no future," Ilse said.

"How can there be no future?"

"Because there is no past," Ilse said, getting up, feeling better, if not stronger. "There is only now."

"I don't understand."

"Where's yesterday?"

"What do you mean where's yesterday?"

Ilse pointed everywhere. "Is the future or the past to the right or to the left? Are they 10 feet away or 10,000 miles in the other direction? I mean, we speak of time as if it were a location."

"What is it then?"

Ilse took Shelby to the window and said, "See that building across the street."

"What about it?"

"It was built what, 50 years ago? But it doesn't exist 50 years ago. It only exists now, otherwise it wouldn't be here; it would only be *there*, 50 years ago. That is what I learned over *there*."

"And that old lady?"

Ilse said, "She showed me some spooky wooden masks."

"Why?"

"I don't know why, but as I reached for one, she said, 'Now is not the time.'"

"Why not?"

"I don't know," Isle said. "But this whole notion that life on earth is a continual process of going into the future is screwy, because we're not going anywhere."

"Then where *are* we going?"

"Nowhere."

"How can that be?"

Ilse said, "Because what we're really doing is constantly creating conditions based on what we want or want to avoid, and in that tension, we experience the illusion of time going forward, in the same way we experience time going nowhere when we're just sitting around doing nothing—but that is not time. What is really being measured is what you're doing, and the name given for it is time—and the consequence of those actions become experience, and to retain it we create new experiences. That is why we are down here, and for that alone. The question should be 'Are you experienced?', not 'What time is it?'"

"What if you're wrong?"

"What if I'm right......?

31

Sigmaringen

The hard rain made waste of the Black Forest's winding roads. Visibility was a matter of nerve as a spinout would send you into the thorny grip of the ever-looming Schwarzwald. Arno Krückel, the driver, used the odometer of his 1923 Torpedo Hansa Type 3 to keep time in these hilly regions of Bavaria scattered with ancient towns and fortresses built right alongside mountains, rivers, and valleys. Road lights were nonexistent, and monotony monitored the second hand. Arno Krückel said to Hugo Schultheiß in the passenger seat, "Are we there yet?"

"Just about," Hugo Schultheiß said, looking up from under his hat.

"How much more to go?"

"Check the odometer."

"I just did," Arno Krückel said.

"Then we shouldn't be far."

A muffled noise came from the back seat.

Arno Krückel glanced into the rear-view mirror and said, "Maybe we should take the gag off her now."

"It stays on," Hugo Schultheiß said, as he kept his eyes on the road ahead. "…There it is."

"What is?"

"The turnoff."

"I can't see it," Arno Krückel said.

"It's just past the road sign."

"What road sign?"

"The one up ahead."

Arno Krückel saw nothing but the clacking of windshield wipers that interfered with his vision.

Hugo Schultheiß reached over and forced a hard-right turn that broke the forest's spell. The light, from the town of Sigmaringen, gave shape to the Danube River along the embankment. High above the cliffs stood the ancient castle under the moon's chill. Its medieval spires and massive perch were over 700 years old. The Torpedo Hansa crossed the old bridge that arched the Danube and rode up the steep hill to the fortress. It stopped short of a huge portcullis flanked by towers with arrow loops that had been modified for rifles. Arno Krückel held a flashlight outside the window. He signaled the watchtower where princes once kept view as others mounted coups. He said to Hugo Schultheiß, "We're late. Maybe they've given up on us."

"No one's given up," Hugo Schultheiß said.

Then the heavy portcullis was raised, and the Torpedo drove into the castle's bailey. Two party men greeted them and took Zola out of the car, one of them saying, "And where's Hugenberg?"

"He wasn't at home," Hugo Schulthieß said.

"Then he was either lucky or had been informed……"

32

The Eastern Bloch

Emil Hugenberg met Al Nachman at the foot of the *Bismarck* Memorial statue that stood in front of the imposing Reichstag where all the parties of government sat in Berlin. Al greeted him and said to him in German, "What brings us here?"

"I've been up all night, but that's another matter."

"Something wrong?"

"There's always something wrong," Emil Hugenberg said.

"Why did you want to meet here of all places?"

"I asked you to come here, because the last time we met I felt that you didn't understand my situation," Emil Hugenberg said as he looked up at the looming statue of Otto von Bismarck with his cuirassier pickelhaube helmet and longhorn mustache. "Back in the 1890s, my generation held the future of the world since Germany was then—and still is—the leader in science and technology. People to this very day are coming from all over the world to study here despite the fact that we unfairly lost our self-respect because of the war, and we feel this deep pain every time someone looks at us and sees only evil. The world has painted a picture of us that is unfair and full of lies. We are good people and yet you treat us like dogs, especially the French. They spit and kick at a man down on his knees and then make him pay what he has not, and because of this there is widespread resentment in our country that is only growing…Yes, the war was madness, and we were all responsible for the disaster, but for the English and French to rewrite history and put the blame solely on us, just shows you that evil and sainthood are bred from the same mothers. Nevertheless, I did not invite you here just to tell you that," Emil Hugenberg said as he took a frayed book out of his coat pocket and showed it to Al. "There once was an industrialist named Bloch, from Poland, who in the late 1890s had seen the future of the world with unparalleled clarity and he published this vision in a book titled the *Future of War*. Word for word, he laid out the industrial violence that was on the way: rapid firing machine guns, devastating artillery that would cause entrenchment and stalemate, and the complete industrialization of warfare into an attritional killing machine.

"He handed out his book to all the statesmen, generals, kings, even the Czar, those men still steeped in the glory of cavalry charges and splendid uniforms, but the old order refused to listen to him because he had dared to warn them of the devastation to come and the revolutions that would topple Europe's monarchies. Bloch laid it out word for word and in precise detail backed by figures instead of the usual political rhetoric that is dumped like shit on the human mind as in Hitler's *Mein Kampf.* Despite this, or maybe because of this, everyone resented Bloch for trying to be rational with his irrefutable facts and industrial production figures which he used to show how total war would invariably spiral out of control and kill millions and millions of people. I was even offered the book to publish, but I saw it as garbage. As far as I was concerned, Bloch was just one of those irritating rich men who'd been taken in by poets and dreamers cheated of fame by their own reckless poverty and personal misgivings…Now, you may ask, why do I bring this up? Well, I've only just read the book. You see, an acquittance of mine, by the name of Manfred Pschorr, sent it to me along with a note about Hitler's *Mein Kamp* that said, 'When bullshit turns into political orthodoxy, then we're all screwed.' … I'm afraid he's correct, Mr. Nachman. And, after reading *The Future of War*, I was stunned by the clarity and ability of Bloch, a Jew, to make his case using precedence, facts, and figures, well in advance of the coming catastrophe. In fact, his wasn't even a prediction, he had just opened his eyes, as mine are now open about the impending doom if we continue on this way, and that is why I can't let Major Coors nor anyone else get that shipment of munitions…Having said that, I will have to deny any word you say about our conversation, and I will pretend to continue to support these fools, only for the safety of my family. Please see me as a friend in need, who may soon need to ask you a favor."

"You're a hypocrite then."

Emil Hugenberg waved for his car and said, "Herr Nachman, see me as one who understands the protection that hypocrisy can offer." He got into his car and was whisked away. Al found a public telephone and called Beau who said, "I just spoke to Shelby. She's at Ilse Dietrich's apartment. The Major beat Ilse. I was just on my way there now."

Al said, "Call them and tell them to stay put and let no one in the apartment. We'll get to them shortly, but first, I need you to meet me at the Gipsdiele Tavern right off Alexander Platz……"

33

The Cigar Box

The Gipsdiele Tavern was located in a run-down quarter north of Alexander Platz where immigrants from the east flooded the side streets with cluttered carts of used goods that had been discarded, abandoned, or stolen. This wasn't lost on Beau as he entered the dive. Several of the patrons were using tabletops for pillows and all of them were the thick of the city's lard: the part of the beast where the meat is always hard to get at. One of them, just waking up, stared at Beau, wondering what a black man was doing there. So did the pimp standing by the clock that competed with the boredom of mid-morning. Beau walked past the collage of misery and continued on into the backroom where the light, moist with low wattage, couldn't hide the layers of grime chronicling the years of filth, but then maybe it was just the water shortage which had kept the mop off the floor. He took the chair across from Al, who said to him, "Any problem getting here?"

"No, took the train to Alexander Platz and walked up the street," Beau said, looking around. "I been to juke joints in Clarksdale higher class than this hole in the wall."

"I have no doubt. You've got the camera?"

Beau patted the side of his overcoat.

"Heard anything from Sarah Remley?"

"No one has," Beau said.

"When was the last time she was at the hotel?"

"Right before she went to see that cousin of hers, von Remmele, in Grunewald."

"Do you know anything about the two men who tried to pick the lock of her room the other day?"

"I heard from Mr. Benchley that they got away; that's all," Beau said, as he watched a cockroach on the floor change direction.

"So, where in Bavaria are you going?"

"Small town called Sigmaringen, where Ziggy, the manager of the cabaret, comes from."

"And the Major as well."

"Yep, and he gonna be there too," Beau said, "but then plans always change and what comes next don't always care what happened last, but I'll be there to find out."

"Well, the town of Sigmaringen just happens to be the seat of the Catholic branch of the Hohenzollern Royal family."

"What of it?"

Al said, "The Kaiser was from the Protestant Hohenzollern branch. His line had all the power—or they did. The Catholic side has blamed them for the loss of the monarchy."

"And the Major is from the Catholic side?"

"So it seems," Al said. "Now, what about Ziggy?"

"Her real name is Elfriede. Ziggy is short for Sigmaringen where she comes from. Even her brother calls her that."

"Well, I got a feeling this trip of yours may be more than just about Fastnacht," Al said, as he took notice of a middle-aged man, short and muscular, wearing a worn wool overcoat and cap that hid the part of his face that told the truth. He took the opposite table against the wall. Al said, "Get your camera ready."

The woman behind the bar came into the backroom and put a stein of beer beside the man's cigar box.

Al said to Beau, in a low voice, "That's Klopp, the thief who burgled Shelby with Ilse Dietrich. That's why he carries the cigar box. Now, I paid off the house dick to get his name and some other useful information."

"Does Klopp know we're here?"

"Well, I paid the barmaid off too," Al said, "so that he wouldn't."

"She the one who contacted him for you?"

"Yeah," Al said.

"Maybe he paid her off to find out who you are?"

"Maybe," Al said.

"What about that cigar box?"

"It's the sign of a professional thief," Al said. "They keep their tools in it. Have you got the shutter speed and f-stop set for low lighting?"

"Already done."

"Good," Al said. "I'm going to walk over there and say hello. When Klopp looks up, get a picture of him, and then leave. I'll meet you down the block as soon as I'm done."

"What do you plan on doing with his photo?"

"Scare the shit out of him, once it's developed," Al said.

"How you gonna to do that?"

"At the right time, I'll give it to the press with the story about his connection to the Black Reichswehr and Major Coors and the hotel thefts. You see, the police could've thrown him in jail for years, but they didn't."

"Why not?"

"I would guess to keep an eye on him," Al said, getting up and walking over to the burglar's table.

Klopp looked up at the tall red blooded American full of beer, butter, and beef, and wondered what the hell he was doing in Deutschland. Al picked up the cigar box and said to Klopp in German, "If you or anyone else tries to steal anything from those two American women, again, you're a dead man."

"…Who are you?"

"The son of a bitch that'll kill you."

Click.

34

Love Letters

On their way back from Alexander Platz, the hotel concierge handed Beau a sealed envelope. He read it and showed it to Al who said, "Were you in your room when I left earlier to meet Hugenberg?"

"No, I went out to check the cafés and other places for Mrs. Remley. I got the call from Shelby when I got back, but I never got this note, because I never give my room key to the concierge."

"We'll call her now." They entered Al's room and when Ilse picked up, Al introduced himself and then said, "Is Shelby there?"

"She's with me now," Ilse said.

"I've got some crazy note here that says she's been kidnapped."

"I know all about it," Ilse said. "I was at the Red Castle this morning."

"What were you doin' over there?"

"There's an Inspector Degler who wants me to get him a certain letter of release. He said that Shelby had been kidnapped, which she wasn't."

"How well do you know Klopp?"

"…You know him?"

"Of him," Al said.

"He's a master burglar."

"Does he have a political agenda?"

"Money is his agenda," Ilse said, "but he hates the communists because in the fighting days he lost a brother to them."

"How long has he been working for von Coors?"

"As long as he gets paid," Ilse said.

"Is Klopp dangerous?"

"They all are," Ilse said. "Violence is no big deal for those who were in the war."

"What do you mean?"

Ilse said, "You remember that scandal about the ambassador and that prostitute whom they found dead?"

"I hadn't gotten here, yet."

"Well, they were writing love letters in English and my job was to translate them into German to put the dirt on the ambassador. Then the whore was found murdered, and the Ambassador was in the hot seat."

"Klopp stole the letters?"

"Yeah," Ilse said, "which were then handed over to the newspapers and then the ambassador committed suicide, but I don't believe that."

"You mean Klopp killed him."

"No," Ilse said, "but he got into where the whore lived and made it look like the ambassador killed her by leaving their stolen love letters at her place. You see, when he had gotten tired of her, she tried to extort money from him, and so he threw her a bone now and then until he told her to get lost."

"What did the nationalists have against the ambassador?"

"He was tied in with the Soviets," Ilse said, "and was funneling money to the Reds over here, or at least that's what's claimed."

"Why were you there?"

"I wasn't," Ilse said.

"So, then, how do you know all this?"

Ilse said, "Because the killer and I are friends and he told me that the girl had a funny little mouth that looked even funnier after he choked her to death."

"…How many friends of yours are killers?"

"Not many," Ilse said.

"You say that rather casually."

"Look, the front-line soldiers who came home from the war are all used to death, so what was once forbidden is now common—and who did the kidnappers get if it wasn't Shelby?"

"I'm not sure, yet," Al said. "Have you heard from Zola?"

"No one ever knows where she is."

"Well, I'll be over soon enough to find Shelby a safe place."

"Well, between you and me," Ilse said, "there's nowhere safe in Germany......"

Ten minutes later, a woman with a windswept bob turned the key to her room.

"Mrs. Remley...?"

She turned around to look at the stranger who had appeared behind her in the corridor and said, "Who are you?"

"My name is Al Nachman. This is my associate, Beau LaHood.

"Associate...?"

"Yes. I'm a lawyer from Mississippi that does special criminal investigative work."

"I thought he was Shelby's servant."

"He was," Al said.

"Does Shelby know that?"

"Not yet."

Sarah turned to Beau and said, "I can't wait to see the look on her face."

"I wouldn't worry about that," Al said. "Now, Beau was under the impression that you were missing."

"I was detained."

"By whom?"

"At the Red Castle."

"You were arrested?"

"Not exactly," Sarah said.

"I suppose they wanted that letter of release."

"I see you know about it," Sarah said. "Would you two like to come in?"

"If we could have a few words." Once inside Al said, "So, what were you doing at the Red Castle?"

Sarah said, "To make a long story short, I told the police that I didn't have any kind of letter, but I made a deal with them."

"What kind of deal?"

"To keep an eye on things," Sarah said. "Let them know of anything that might be of interest to them."

"Such as your cousin Egon von Remmele," Al said.

"Him and other things, and that seemed more than enough for the police, at least for now. Have you seen Zola?"

"Why?"

Sarah said, "It seems the Political Division has files on her. Some of them rather juicy but, being a lady, I shall refrain from going into detail. They're looking for her as well."

"Do you have the letter of release on you?"

"Mr. Nachman, you are aware of the mail thefts here."

"I've been informed."

"Well," Sarah said, "I can assure you that no one will find anything on me."

Al said, "Are you prepared to deal with the consequences should anyone try to get a hold of you?"

"You mean kidnap me?"

"That or something else," Al said, as they turned in response to a knock at the door.

Sarah opened the door and said, "I thought we were done for the day."

You and I are," Inspector Degler said, accompanied by two assistant inspectors. He then showed his badge to Al and said in German, "Are you Alton Nachman?"

"Yes, and who are you?"

Inspector Degler said, "Come with me, please."

"Why?"

"I'll explain on the way," said the inspector.

"On the way to where?"

"To headquarters."

"On what grounds?"

"Mr. Nachman, when the Berlin police invite you for little a chat, take it as a compliment." The inspector pointed the way.

Al turned to Beau and said in English. "Take the train to the port now and don't wait."

"You mean what we talked about on our way back from Alexander Platz?"

"Yes."

"What about Shelby?"

"They kidnapped the wrong girl," Al said. "In fact, I think it's a diversion for what's going on in that port, so you better hurry."

The inspector interrupted Al and said, "If you have anything to say, say it in German, or remain quiet."

"And just how long are you going to detain me, if that's even legal?"

Inspector Degler said, "Now, that's a good question......"

35

Togoland

Beau bought the train ticket to Hamburg from the hotel's railroad office and then called Shelby. She said to him, "Well, before you leave, hide my gun and an extra round of cartridges in my clothing, and have them all sent over to Ilse's apartment through an outside courier service and not the hotel's. Now, when are you leaving?"

Beau said, "Next train is not for another two hours or so, because of a delay. I could stop over in the meantime."

"No, don't miss the train. You have to get to Hamburg. Just make sure that my gun is sent over."

"Consider it done, miss."

"And congratulations on your new job......"

Early that evening Beau took a taxi over to the Lehrter Bahnof where he boarded a steam locomotive train for Hamburg. He shared a compartment with a man who was nodding off and losing grip of his newspaper. A woman opened the door and said to Beau, in German, "Would you mind if I take that empty seat?"

Beau didn't understand her, so she said it in English. He said, "Help yourself, ma'am."

"Why thank you, sir. I'm Honora Bekendorp. A pleasure to meet you."

"A pleasure to meet you, ma'am. You speak English well."

"My mother was from England. Your name, sir?"

"Joe."

"Joe who?"

"Joe Nobody."

"That can't be your name," Honora Bekendorp said.

"That's what it is, ma'am."

"Well, if you say so." She sat down and made herself comfortable. "Now, what brings you to Germany all the way from America?"

"I'm a musician. And you?"

Honora Bekendorp said, "My late husband was German, and his family has a very prosperous trading company located in Hamburg. Unfortunately, when he died his brother inherited the business and bought out all our shares and then tried to disown me and my children, so I've got some unfinished business with him, which is why I'm on my way to Hamburg. Do you have lodgings there, Mr. Nobody?"

"I do."

"Where?"

Beau said, "I'll be staying at a hotel."

"Well, how nice. So am I," Honora Bekendorp said as she made herself comfortable. "Now, I don't mean to be impolite, but you're the first black American I've ever met, but then I haven't been to America myself. So, why are you going to Hamburg?"

"See some friends," Beau said.

"How nice. Where do they live?"

"St. Pauli district."

"The St. Pauli district?"

"Yes, ma'am."

"And that's where you're going?"

"I'm about to," said Beau.

"They say that the district is—"

"What...?"

"You know."

"No, I don't know," Beau said.

"They call it the sinful mile."

"You been there?"

"I've been around there, certainly not *in* there," she said.

"What's so sinful about it?"

"Well, Mr. Nobody, it would be difficult to explain in polite company." She left it at that.

Beau didn't. "What would be so difficult?"

"It's where they do those things."

"Do what things?"

"Things one shouldn't," Honora Bekendorp said leaning back and giving herself a quick fan. "Forgive me, but I've had a long day and it would be impolite of me to continue talking when I'm not my full self." She turned away from Beau, but he could see that she was trembling as she searched her bag for a small vial that she bit on and poured down her mouth. The shaking soon subsided. She then said to Beau, "Malaria. I used to live in the jungle." She then shut her eyes and soon fell asleep.

When they arrived in Hamburg, they shared a taxi to the Hotel St. Petersburg. Beau signed in, went to his room, and thought of what Al had told him on their way back from the Gipsdiele: "Go to Hamburg and to the maze of warehouse buildings in and about the Speicherstadt canals that border the St. Pauli district and Hafencity. It may seem dark and gloomy at night, but don't let that bother you. Find the *Pegasus*, because it's moved since I left, and then keep an eye out for anything or anyone out of the ordinary and take photos like you did back in Manhattan's Meat District. Of course, if you find yourself in another situation, stay with it, as it might become your real lead. Once you're done, return to Berlin."

Beau loaded Al's Leica 1A with 35mm film and wound it to the first frame. He took several ACP .45 clips that were hidden in his Gladstone bag and slipped it inside his suit jacket along with his Colt. There was a knock on the door. "Who is it?"

"Honora Bekendorp—we met on the train. I do hope I'm not catching you at the wrong time, Mr. Nobody."

Beau put on his overcoat and opened the door. There she was all dolled up in a navy-blue knee length white fox fur collar coat and a matching cloche with staggered Art Deco silver and gold tracing."

Beau said, "Actually, I'm on my way out."

"So am I, Mr. Nobody."

"Yeah, but I have to meet up with some folks now."

"In the St. Pauli district?"

"Possibly," Beau said, locking the door to his hotel room and then heading down the hallway. "You goin' to a party, ma'am?"

"No. Are you?"

"As I said, I have to visit friends."

"Any one in particular?"

"Some sailors," Beau said.

"My brother was a sailor."

"Maybe I'll run into him."

"No, I don't think so," Honora Bekendorp said as she tagged along. "He was on the Indefatigable that went down at the Battle of Jutland."

"Sorry to hear that, ma'am," Beau said as he took notice of the splendid ornate carpet and old-world trimmings of the hotel. He turned into the central hallway and continued on under the bright light of the grand chandelier.

Honora Bekendorp was right beside him. "Do you know which is my favorite cabaret in Berlin?"

"I don't have a clue, ma'am."

"Take a guess," she said.

"There's a lot of 'em, ma'am.

"Der Himmel u. Hölle Kabarett."

"That's nice."

"Have you ever been there?"

"Been to a lot of joints in Berlin," Beau said.

"Then I'll refresh your memory—it's where you played the saxophone."

Beau stopped and said, "You just remembered that, or did it somehow slip your mind on the train?"

"Well, not at first, no," Honora Bekendorp said, as Beau went on down the grand stairway to the lobby and then out of the hotel and into the lavish loggia, which extended to the bay where passenger jitneys were docked. "Where are we going, Mr. Nobody?"

"I didn't know you was comin' along," Beau said as he continued on down the road, past the jitneys. He took out his map.

"Don't worry, you're going the right way," Honora Bekendorp said, letting Beau know that he didn't need the map as long as she was there. "I hope you aren't upset at me for trying to be of some help."

"…You're a very nice person, ma'am."

"Good. Now which club are we going to? I suppose you have one all picked out."

"Just goin' to see some friends, ma'am. That's all."

"Well, I've been to all the cabarets in Berlin. One has to keep up with everything, now that I'm not married and free as a bird."

"You sure it's proper for a lady to be goin' out at night all by herself?"

"Don't be silly," Honora Bekendorp said, as they crossed the street. "I'm with you."

"You are…?"

"Yes, Mr. Nobody—that is unless you really don't like me and want to hurt my feelings. I'll go right back to the hotel and cry all by myself."

Beau just stared at her.

"And remember, Mr. Nobody, that I speak German, you don't, and that I'm well educated, despite my late husband's corrupt brother who thinks I'm a dummkopf."

"Yeah, but I'm black. You're white. Could be trouble."

"Don't be silly. Should anyone ask why you're with me, why you just tell them that you're my servant from Togoland and they'll completely understand."

"…Togoland?"

"One of our former colonies. Now, what kind of girl are you looking for?"

"I ain't lookin' for any," Beau said.

"You're looking for a boy?"

"No, ma'am, I most certainly ain't."

"Proper men always pretend to be shy, but it would behoove you to know that every street whore in the district has a pimp and if he thinks that you're some hayseed from Togoland then he's going to take advantage of you. So, I'll negotiate for you, make sure you get a nice girl at a fair price—unless you want a boy."

"Look ma'am, I don't want no one and I ain't from Togoland. I'm from the United States of America, a country that I love even though it don't love me back."

"Well, don't let that worry you," Honora Bekendorp said. "Maybe we can stumble upon one of those cute little cabarets where mixed people go to dance. I'm a very good dancer. I can do the Charleston magnificently and the Fox Trot as smooth as spread butter. How about you?"

"My feet don't move that fast," Beau said as they reached the Elbe River where the docks and warehouses stood as far as the eye could see. Ships of all sizes crammed the ports and canals with smoke stacks, rounded sterns, and edged bows that lunged into the sky. Beer joints were rooted into narrow lanes next to clubs that seemed more makeshift than permanent. Whores drifted by and gave Beau a name so that when they came back for a second try, they would seem like old friends. Beau noticed some African sailors coming along, who spoke in the equatorial octave. They advised him to go to the infamous Indian Bar, as it was patronized by sailors of color and that he would find good company there—Honora Bekendorp did all the translating. Beau thanked them and then said to Honora Bekendorp, "You seem to be at home here."

"I'm comfortable anywhere, Mr. Joe Nobody, and I've already told you that I've lived around the world."

"Oh, you mean Africa."

"Yes, Africa, that spread of earth with its vicious cold-blooded snakes such as the Gaboon Viper with its murderously long fangs or those damned Black Mambas that slither as fast as a horse and then spit in your eyes and leave you blind unless you quickly wash out their poison with urine, and if you don't, you will die a horrifying death. I even killed a man one night, but I don't want to ruin the evening talking about a fool who had no honor."

"You killed a man…?"

"You won't hear it from him," Honora Bekendorp said with her nose high up in the air.

"You oughta visit America then," Beau said.

"Why?"

"Kinda like Africa."

"How so?"

"We got our own nasty Mambas, but they ain't black."

They went on through the maze of ports and canals in and around the St. Pauli District and neighboring Hafencity, and then into the narrow waterways that were crammed with cargo ships and ocean liners that bulged in the tight canals. Flags flew from as far away as Japan and the Horn of Africa. During the day tugboats, barges, and rows of high swinging cranes cranked boxed goods into bales of nets that were hoisted from the wharves and then down into the depths of the cargo holds. A maze of brick warehouses and narrow dark streets stored dry goods and coolers for skinned pigs. Honora Bekendorp said to Beau, "So what's the name of the ship that your friends are on?"

"I didn't give it."

"Well, how're are we going to find it? I mean, we've been going around in circles like a bunch of fools. I don't know why it's such a secret."

"I never said I was lookin' for a ship," Beau said.

"Then why are we here…? Now, which ship are you looking for?"

Overwhelmed by the immensity of the port and the need to not waste any more time, Beau said, "…The *Pegasus.*"

Honora Bekendorp stopped a sailor across the way and asked him where the *Pegasus* could be found. He pointed toward the Speicherstadt area and said that the freighter had to be by the Grasbrookhafen and if not there then the Landsungbrüken. She and Beau continued on through the high mounted cranes and crammed docks until they reached Grasbrookhafen. A little later, Honora Bekendorp pointed up ahead and said. "There it is." It took a moment for Beau to make it out, but then he saw the carved magnolias high up on the prow. He took out his camera. Honora Bekendorp said to him, "Don't you think it's a bit too dark to take pictures?"

"I'm dark, so it ain't a problem."

"Yes, but why are you taking pictures?"

"Because I'm crazy," Beau said as he set the f-stop of the Leica Model 1A to 3.5, low as it could go, and aimed the lens at a group of men standing by the cargo warehouse opposite the ship. *Click*. A moment later one of the Germans approached him and said something that made all the others laugh. Honora Bekendorp reproached them and then said to Beau, "You shouldn't be taking their photograph."

"What did he say?"

"That it's not decent to just take someone's photo without informing him."

"What did you tell him?"

"That you're my servant and to mind their own business."

Beau then noticed several trucks coming down the road. They parked perpendicular to the ship. *Click*. He crossed the pier and stopped at the gangway of the *Pegasus* and said to Honora Bekendorp, "This is where our journey ends, but thanks for all the help and maybe I'll see you one day in Berlin." He headed up the gangway but was stopped by an American sailor. "Who goes there?"

"Beau LaHood. I'm here to see the captain."

"Who's the white woman?"

"I'm his translator," Honora Bekendorp said, catching up, and then to Beau, "I thought your name was Joe Nobody."

Beau said to her, "It's getting' late, ma'am. Better be goin' back to the hotel. I won't be needin' a translator, now."

She took a hanky from her coat and cried into it. "And I've tried to be so nice to you and you just want to be mean to me."

Beau ignored her.

The sailor hung up the ship's telephone that was fixed on the bulwark and said to Beau, "Go to the end of the deck and take the ladder straight up."

Honora Bekendorp searched herself and said to Beau, "I can't find it."

"Find what?"

"My purse."

"I don't think you had one," Beau said.

"Don't be silly, of course I had one." She scavenged through the pockets of her coat. "I…I must've dropped it on the way here." She hurried down the gangway and looked everywhere. A man on the dock, came up to her and handed her the purse. Beau immediately recognized him and aimed his camera at Klopp. *Click.* He then continued on to the foreword deck where he found Captain Ellsworth Marsham in the wheelhouse. "Excuse me, Captain, I'm Beau LaHood, an associate of Al Nachman."

The captain said, "Yes, he told me all about you, Beau. Welcome aboard. This is First Officer Shoney. The first officer and Beau shook hands. The captain then said to Beau on their way out of the wheelhouse, "There's a bit of a chill tonight. I'll have some coffee and rum brought up from the galley to my cabin."

"That's exactly what I need," Honora Bekendorp said, coming down the deck and out of breath.

Before they reached the cabin, Beau took Captain Ellsworth Marsham to the side and said, "Sir, I need you to help me get rid of that woman."

"I was told that she was your translator."

"She ain't my nothin'," Beau said. "I just saw a man named Klopp on the dock who works for the DNF, one of the nationalist factions who want what's on this boat, and I have no doubt that that woman has somethin' to do with it, and now she inside your cabin."

"Then we'll get her off…"

But it wasn't so easy to do. Honora Bekendorp's bobbed wig was on the deck of the captain's cabin. She, or he, was sighting an Ortgies .38 Automatic dead on them. Beau said to the now familiar face, "Didn't you work the door at the Silhouette, that transvestite cabaret, in Berlin?"

"I still do," the former Honora Bekendorp said, but in a deeper voice.

"You was always wearin' men's' clothes then."

"At the door, yes."

"And you're real name's Ulrich."

"It's not my only name, as you now know."

"How did you know I was goin' to Hamburg?"

Ulrich said, "We paid off the railroad agent at your hotel to notify us if any of you were coming here."

"And how did you know which hotel?"

Ulrich smiled, "You were followed from the Gipsdiele." He then turned to the captain. "Give me the keys to the cargo hold."

"I don't have them," the captain said.

"You have the keys and I want them," Ulrich said.

"You certainly won't get them if you kill me."

Ulrich stepped back and opened the porthole behind him, and without turning he waved a bright green handkerchief through it and said to the captain, "Very soon this ship will be overtaken. Now give me the keys or you *will* die."

Captain Ellsworth Marsham said, "The keys are in Berlin. So, you and your friends might as well go home."

"The keys are *here*," Ulrich said.

"You have no grounds to believe that," said the captain.

The sound of gunfire was heard below deck.

Ulrich said, "I want those keys, or you'll be hearing more than gunfire."

"I don't have them."

"You're lying, Captain. They're in this cabin."

"And what makes you think that?"

Ulrich said, "Because if a fire or an emergency happens on board ship it would be a long walk to Berlin, and no captain would hide them anywhere but in his cabin, where no one is allowed."

"And just what makes you think that?"

"U-Boat service. Now hand them over."

Beau said to Ulrich, "Just so you know, I'm the one who's got the letter of release for that arms shipment down below in the cargo hold, so don't waste your time killin' anyone."

"You've got it on you?"

"And the keys right here inside my coat pocket," Beau said, "and all ya gotta do is present the letter to the port master and every handgun, every box of semi-automatics, machine guns, grenades, and the hundreds of thousands of rounds of ammunition that Uncle Sam made for Uncle Fritz is all yours."

"Give them to me," Ulrich said, putting the Ortgies .38 on Beau.

"Under one condition."

"You don't make conditions here," Ulrich said, extending the automatic.

"Okay, you the boss. I know when the game's over," Beau said, as he reached inside his overcoat. "And you can tell Klopp that he's a lot smarter than we thought."

"He already knows that," Ulrich said, as the expression on his face went from I'm-in-charge to I've-been-had, and by someone who was a lot smarter than he had thought. Ulrich fell hard onto the deck. His wig, dress, and T-straps beside him, were now as mismatched as the life that had left him. Beau put the Colt back into its shoulder holster and said to the captain, "Where are the keys?"

Captain Ellsworth Marsham, with no time to waste, opened a hidden panel behind a writing desk that was attached to the bulkhead. He reached inside it and took out a metal box and gave it to Beau.

"This is yours now."

The gunfire below got louder.

"I want you to leave the ship and get this to Al Nachman."

"What about you, sir?"

"Don't worry about me, Beau."

"You're not going to stay here, are you?"

"A captain does not leave his ship. Now follow me. We have no time to waste."

Beau followed the captain to the end of passageway as the gangway had already been taken over by armed men. "Is there another way off this boat?"

"Yes," said the captain.

"Where?"

"Overboard."

"Overboard…? I wouldn't last five minutes in that frigid water."

Captain Marsham said, "You won't last two minutes if you stay on board with the key box. Now, there's a ladder attached to the side of the next dock. All you have to do is swim to it and you're free. It's not that far."

"You done it before?"

"No," said the captain. "You'll be the first one—or the last."

Beau took another look at the Elbe River, so long and so wide, and began to have second thoughts. "You sure you don't wanna come along?"

"If a captain leaves his ship, then he's leaving more than that."

Beau understood and shook his hand, "God be with you, Cap'n." He then climbed down the ladder to the foredeck and continued on toward the prow that was so high off the water that he felt that he could reach up and touch the sky. He put the camera and Colt into the metal box with the keys and removed his overcoat as it would be dead weight in the water. He then inched over toward the bow and tucked the key box under his arms and held it close against his chest as he balanced one foot on the very edge of the ship to steady himself. He didn't want to think of home, his children, that crazy day in Clarksdale that got him to where he was now, but the thoughts came anyway, and to get away from them he pushed himself off the edge of the ship and went into a freefall that for a few spare seconds separated him from earth, until he collided with the Elbe River where the crush of frigid water slammed hard against his body. He plunged so far down into the river that he had to crawl his way back up, one arm gripping the key box, and as he resurfaced, he realized that the distance to the next dock was something that he could have walked in no time, but then this was water, and he wasn't biblical magic. He was just Beau.

36

The Keeper of Keys

The weight of induced sleep slowly wore off as the drowsy tide of dreams faded and the castle tower's cold stone floor greeted Zola. Bleary eyed and groggy, she sat up and listened to the steady beat of heavy shoes climbing up the tower's stone stairway. She heard the jangling of keys and the groan of the ancient lock that opened the medieval oak plank door that was joined by iron studs and long strap hinges. A low-lit man, seasoned by the darkest parts of the castle, stood in the doorway with a tray in hand. Zola, freezing and in her négligée, pleaded in German, "Where're my clothes?"

The man seemed to be hard of hearing as he set a tray with two slices of pumpernickel bread and a ramekin of butter on the cold stone floor along with a thin glass of water.

Zola vainly tried to warm herself by stroking her bare arms with her hands. "At least tell me who are you."

The man looked up at the fading light that filtered through the slit in the tower wall and said, "The clouds are getting dark."

"I don't care. Where's my clothing? And what am I doing here?"

"Soon it will come."

"My clothes…?"

"Fastnacht," said the man.

Zola knew from his accent that he was Bavarian. She decided to speak with authority as Germans never question someone who convincingly displays it. "*Where* exactly, in Bavaria, are we?"

"I can see it," he said, his eyes on the hypnotic beam of light that filtered through the tower slit.

"See what?"

"Soon it will be," he said.

"What will be?

"The hour."

"What hour?"

"I do not make the spells," he said.

"What're you talking about?"

"She does," he said, turning away.

"*Who* does…?"

"You wear the mask of the person who comes back to life and when the chimes of midnight ring, the sky will part."

"What're you talking about?"

"Over there," he said, pointing to the wall as if he could see through it.

"Where over there?"

"Where death is a mask that you use to see into life, and life is a mask that you can't see out of, except for Fastnacht when anyone who can see will see everything."

"And I suppose you can see."

His eyes lit up. "Maybe that's why you're here."

"Why am I here?"

"I'm not supposed to talk to you," he said turning away.

"Who said that you couldn't?"

He pointed down at the floor.

"Are you a servant?"

"Yes."

"How many servants are there here?"

"Many," he said.

"How many is many?"

"I've always worked in the old part of the castle."

"Which part are we in now?"

"The tower," he said.

"Where…?"

"The old part."

Zola lied, "…You do know that I'm a princess."

He studied her face for a moment.

She tried to stand up. "They didn't tell you that because they don't trust you."

"You speak with an accent."

"I'm a Dutch princess."

"Dutch?"

"Yes."

He said, "I remember when Dutch royalty came here to hunt with the Kaiser before the war."

"Then you must know my grandmother," Zola said.

"Your grandmother…?"

"The Princess of Pyrmont. Very pretty and tall. She danced so very well. She and the Kaiser sang Erlkönig in the Grand Salon."

"Did they…?"

"Did you not hear them?"

"No," he said.

"Where in the castle do you work?"

"There are over 300 rooms," he said.

"You work in each one?"

"I have to know each one."

"Why?"

"I'm the Keeper of Keys," he said.

"The what…?"

"The Keeper of Keys. You should know. You're a princess."

"Yes, but we would never call you the Keeper of Keys."

"No…?"

"I'd call you by your name. Now, what does the Keeper of Keys do here? Would it be any different than in my castle?"

The Keeper of Keys said, "He's in charge of all the rooms and must know how to get inside any one of them in a hurry. And only I know this castle inside out."

"You are a remarkable man, sir. I live in a four-room apartment and get lost all the time."

"…I thought you lived in a castle?"

"Well, yes, I do," Zola said, "but you see my apartments are in the northeast section of my tiny 150-room castle. And our Keeper of Keys is a dumbbell. He's always gets lost. That's why I want to hire a man as skilled as you. In fact, I'm going to write the prince here and speak to him about that, but first you must give me the correct spelling of his name so that I don't make an error and insult his highness."

"I better be going," the servant said, looking at his pocket watch. "I have work to do."

"I will pay you twice what the prince pays you."

"Yes, but—it's not the money," the Keeper of Keys said.

"What is it then?"

"This is my home."

"I'll make you a newer and better home," Zola said.

"Yes, but my bloodline, though humble, is the oldest here."

"How old?"

"A thousand years," the Keeper of Keys said.

"Then for the next ten thousand years your bloodline will continue in your new home. Now, I'm freezing. I need my clothing. You *have* to get me my clothing."

"I only do what I'm told," he said.

"*Get* me my clothing."

"I can't."

"You mean you won't."

"I'm just a servant."

"Then tell me which way is the slit in the wall facing?"

The Keeper of Keys looked up and said, "Where the Danube runs blue."

"You mean as in that song of Sigmaringen?"

"I can't sing. I would not know." He stepped outside the tower entrance.

Zola pleaded with him, "Your princess is freezing. She needs her clothing. You must get me my clothing right now or else."

"I'm just a servant," the Keeper of Keys said.

"One that has no heart."

"A servant only needs ears," the Keeper of Keys said, as he locked the ancient medieval door with his jangling keys and then disappeared into the castle.

37

Matchbox

Berlin spared a ray of sunshine for Beau as he got off the train from Hamburg, but the frigid Elbe River had left him aching all over. He had planned on soaking in a hot bath, but when he arrived at the Hotel Esplanade and learned that Al hadn't yet returned, a bath seemed chilly. He called Ilse's apartment several times. No one answered. Then he called Sarah's hotel room. "…Mrs. Remley?"

"Yes. This is she."

"This is Beau LaHood, ma'am. You seen Shelby at all?"

"Well, I haven't *seen* her, if that's what you mean, but I did speak to her last night when I got back, and she wanted to know if you had returned."

"Where are they now?"

"At Ilse's," Sarah said.

"Then I better hurry over. And you might wanna stay put till I get back. I'll explain to you why later and what's been happenin'."

"I'm coming along, Beau."

"Mrs. Remley……"

Beau and Sarah took a taxi to Franken Straße and rang the bell of Ilse's apartment. No one answered, but the front door opened easily. They then went through each room. The bedroom was where the trouble was. Blood on the carpet. A lamp in pieces on the floor. The dressing table overturned. The telephone yanked from the wall. Beau picked up a box of matches that had an illustration of a Bavarian fachwerkhaus, or half-timbered house, with bold lettering underneath: *Deutsches Haus, Sigmaringen.*" He said, "Sigmaringen is where Ziggy and the Major come from and it's where I'll be headin' for Fastnacht."

Sarah took the box of matches from him as they went down the hall and back into the living room where she found an empty tin of Walküre Gold Tip Cigarettes with the image of Brünnhilde and her long flowing hair, winged helmet, and spear in hand.

"Who's Ziggy?"

Beau said, "Major von Coor's sister, manager of the Heaven and Hell Cabaret where Ilse works." He showed the box of matches to Sarah and said, "You know what I'm thinkin'?

Sarah said, "That the girls are in Sigmaringen."

The front door opened. Someone went down the hall to the bedroom.

Beau quietly said to Sarah, "You speak German."

"So…?"

"Go down the hallway and say that you're a neighbor and that you heard some noise and wanted to know what's goin' on."

"You make that sound easy," Sarah said.

"We need to question the person who just walked here in and see iffen we can learn from somethin' from him, and since I don't speak no German—I'll be in the next room over."

"Doing what?"

Beau said, with half a smile, "Hidin'…"

Recklessness is the quickest way to hell, but Sarah embraced it as she entered Ilse's bedroom where she found a man holding a mop and a bucket of water.

"And just who are you?" Sarah said, as he wrung water into the bucket.

He was sure, from her bearing, that she was from the upper-class, despite her foreign accent. "I'm the maintenance man."

"I can see that, but what are you doing here?"

He showed her the mop as if the answer were written on it.

Sarah picked up what was left of the lamp. "Why is everything broken?"

He looked around the bedroom as though everything were in order. Sarah then noticed an NSDAP cloisonné lapel pin on his jacket. She reached into her bag and took out the one that she had found on her cousin's desk in Grunewald and showed it to the man. "When did you last see the girls who were here?"

His eye was on her pin. "Were you sent down here?"

"I most certainly was," Sarah said. "Now, when did you last see them?"

"Well, I didn't really see anyone," he said.

"You either saw them or you didn't."

"Well, there was a problem with the heating, the other day, and I was on my way to the rally and I stopped off here for a brief moment and saw the girl who lives here just in the doorway, but I didn't speak to her, just to her servant. Maybe you should speak to him, ma'am."

"I already have," Sarah lied, "and he knows nothing of this. Who sent you here to clean up?"

The maintenance man said, "Why you don't wear your lapel pin?"

"Because they're made for men's suit jackets. A woman's dress is too delicate, so until the party makes pins for women, I won't be ruining my good clothing." Sarah showed him the cigarette tin and box of matches. "Are these yours?"

"No."

"Who else was here?"

The maintenance man looked at the tin and said, "Some men were here."

"Were they party members?"

"They weren't wearing party pins," he said.

"What were these men doing here?"

"They didn't tell me," he said.

"You mean to tell me that you took orders from people whom you didn't know."

"I was notified," the maintenance man said.

"Who notified you?"

"Herr Fackler."

"Is he from the party?"

"He is," the maintenance man said. "It's a favor we're doing, he said."

"For whom?"

"I don't know."

"And who were the men who were here?"

"One of them was an aristocrat."

"What was his name?"

"I don't know," said the maintenance man. "He'd been in the army; I know that."

"Was he a private?"

"Of course not," said the maintenance man.

"You mean to tell me that you didn't get his name?"

"I didn't ask for it."

"Well, you had to call him something," Sarah said.

"He was man of position. It was obvious."

Sarah again showed the maintenance man the matchbox that Beau had found in the living room. "Did he say anything about Sigmaringen?"

The maintenance man stared at the matchbox and said, "Well, the other two did."

"Which other two?"

"The other two men who were with him."

"What were they doing here?"

The maintenance man said, "They were in a hurry."

"Why?"

"Something about how long it would take to drive there."

"Were they going alone?"

"They didn't tell me," said the maintenance man.

"What were their names?"

"I don't know."

"You mean to tell me that you had no idea to whom you were speaking?"

"He had an awful scar," said the maintenance man.

"Who did?"

"The aristocrat. From his ear to his throat." The maintenance man moved his finger across his face to show her.

"A dueling scar?"

"No, from the war, you know, when the surgeon ties up the face where the bones are missing, and the man had the shakes too."

"Was he a morphine addict?"

The maintenance man said, "Well, I saw him bite into a vial and swallow its contents. Soon his hands were steady again, but then a lot of us who had been wounded take the bite."

"Was he the only addict here?"

"Well, the other two men seemed okay, but you never know. They may have had bitten the pill already."

"You served in the war?"

"Yes," said the maintenance man, "but I made it through. No morphine for me."

"What about the girl who lived here?"

"What about her?"

"Did you know her?"

"The Jewess?"

"How did you know that she was a Jewess?"

"Herr Fackler told me," said the maintenance man.

"Herr Fackler…?"

"From the party."

"The one with the scar?"

"No, he's other one," the maintenance man said.

"You mean Herr Schwab."

"Herr Schwab…?"

"Yes, Herr Schwab. He's the one who's behind this," Sarah said, "and I'll have you know that the girls are not Jewesses."

"That can't be."

"It damn well is, and they're as Aryan as you or I," Sarah said. "It seems that someone is spreading lies against our party. Soon they'll be calling us all Jews."

"I'm not a Jew," said the maintenance man.

"How do I know that?"

"I'll pull down my pants, if I have to."

"I suppose the girls pulled down their pants for you," Sarah said.

"Well, it's different with a woman."

"Yes, it is," Sarah said, "which means that you have no idea what they are."

"I just do what Herr Fackler tells me to do."

"And he does what someone else tells him to do. That's the whole problem," Sarah said. "Next time listen to Herr Schwab." She headed to the door and said, "Finish up cleaning here and then leave." Sarah went down the hallway and found Beau. They slipped out of the apartment and headed back to the hotel. On the way, she said, "When we get back to the hotel, we're packing our bags and taking the next train to Sigmaringen. I'll see if I can get Mr. Benchley to come along with us, as well."

"What for?"

Sarah said, "We'll need a white man with us in case a there are any problems."

"Such as?"

"I think you can guess……"

38

Sigmaringen

Dusk was settling over the small medieval town of Sigmaringen, as the Keeper of Keys lit a candle and sat down beside his wife, Elke, in their castle rooms. She was just waking up. He said to her, "They're on the way."

"…You saw them?"

"Only one," said the Keeper of Keys as he set the candle holder on the nightstand and said, "One day you may not come back from the other side, and I will be left all alone."

"No one dies," Elke said. "The veil of eternity is everywhere; you are already there."

"But you'll be on the other side, and I'll still be here."

"No," Elke said. "The center is wherever you are. Judge not by your eyes."

"But you said in your trance that blood would spill."

"It will," she said.

"Then what about us?"

"What about us?"

The Keeper of Keys said, "The Norns control the destiny of mankind. We just can't make demands."

"The powers are quick to reward those who love them."

"But not those who use them," he said.

"Everyone uses each other, be they Gods or buzzards."

"And should we fail?"

"We fail if we do nothing." Elke said. "Now, when will all three of them be here?"

"Before midnight. They will be put in the tower with the other Norn."

Elke said, "The one in the tower is not a Norn."

"Who is she then?"

"It matters not," Elke said, "but I do see trouble."

"For us…?"

"Trouble for one is trouble for all," Elke said as she headed to the door. "Come. It's time to weave…"

39

Midnight Sleeper

The day slipped away as the midnight sleeper left Berlin and headed south toward Bavaria. Beau said to Sarah, as they entered their compartment, "Maybe I should sleep outside."

"Why would you want to do that?"

"Bein' we booked late, there was nothin' left, but this here one compartment."

"And I suppose that's your fault?"

"No."

"Beau, you are not sitting out in the aisle all night." Sarah then took off her coat and almost tripped. "Why did you bring your saxophone?"

"Ziggy asked me to play for Fastnacht, so I brought it."

"You forget that we have to look for the girls," Sarah said, opening her hand trunk. "Now, we better dress for supper, because the last person served always eats from an empty menu." She fumbled through her clothing.

Beau headed to the door. "I'll step outside, while you change."

"No, I need you here to hang up my things. I have no maids this trip."

Beau kept his eyes away as Sarah undressed, thinking she was no different than a lot of the other white women on the Pullman trains who had no problem with a black man seeing them half naked, as if by race he didn't share the same sentiments as other men.

"Hang this up, please" Sarah said, now in her flimsy silk teddy.

"You know I happen to have a new job," Beau said.

"Just put it behind the other one, the dress with those cubist designs over there."

He did what she said, but his eyes were on her soft shoulders and light brown hair that fluffed off her neck. Sarah then lifted her teddy high over her head and stood naked with her full breasts swaying. "I want that dress over there."

"Uh, which dress, ma'am?"

"The second one," Sarah said.

Beau handed her a diaphanous, sleeveless, scooped neckline beaded chiffon evening dress in light blue that had alternating transparent ball and cylinder beads that streamed down and coiled into florets by the hem. The Nefertiti yoke was made of seven rows of densely clustered beds and when Sarah held it against her chest Beau felt it against his heart.

She said to him, "There's a spot on it right over there. Please get it out." She handed him the dress and then said with a smile, "You know, it's kinda fun being on your own. Don't you think?"

"Fun…?"

"You know. Roughing it up. I'm used to all my maids and comforts. Then my husband got killed and, well, now it's a whole new ballgame as they say."

"How many maids you got, ma'am?"

"I stopped counting years ago," Sarah said, going through the drawers in her trunk. "I had to pack so fast before leaving New York, that I now can't seem to find anything. Shelby had called me out of the blue and I just didn't know what to say or do. I mean, I've never traveled alone in my life, but then how do you say no to a verified flapper? Though I have to admit, it was like jumping into cold water."

"Cold water…?" Beau said, thinking of the Elbe River.

"Very much so, and I believe a little soda water will get this spot out. There's a bottle on the tray right over there."

Beau reached for it, but he was too close to Sarah to not take in her soft pleasure, she who stood before him bare and unashamed, busy with being feminine. He took the soda water and started to rub out the spot. A knock on the compartment door made Sarah cover up. "Who is it?" she said, speaking in authoritative German.

"I have your evening paper as requested," the train steward said.

"I'll have my servant take it," Sarah said, stepping out of view, telling Beau, "Open the door." She then took the paper from him and scanned each page as if her life depended on it.

"Lookin' for somethin', ma'am?"

"I most certainly am……"

40

The Castle

The Keeper of Keys was hiding inside a secret passageway where a gap, hidden by crossed lances, had been chiseled into the wall centuries ago. He kept his eye on the grand winding staircase that was bedecked with mythical statues, taxidermied beasts, and medieval knights either posed in stone or woven into giant tapestries that hung on the walls. One of men coming down the staircase said, "…Well, with her American accent we were sure that she was the right girl, but if you want, I can send Schultheiß and Krückel back to Berlin."

Otto Zumbach, the chief political officer of the DNF, said, "You don't have to. Have you heard from the ship?"

"No, but von Feffenhausen should be here shortly," said another man."

"Good," Otto Zumbach said. "I just hope that he's not as crooked as his face."

The Keeper of Keys watched the men disappear into the main hallway. Then he hurried through the interior passageway back to his rooms. When he reached them, he touched the small carved figurine of the Lutzelfrau that was tacked above the door. Then he entered and walked over to the window overlooking the rolling hills that pitched the quaint little towns up and down the Danube Valley. Life would soon change in this sleepy hamlet, but for the better, he wasn't sure.

41

Schnitzel

Sarah found what she was looking for. She showed the evening newspaper to Beau and said. "This is the letter my late husband had dictated to me in English to translate into German which was then sent to Emil Hugenberg in Berlin."

Beau, leaning over her shoulder, said, "What does it say in English?"

Sarah put down the newspaper and said, "Let me first get dressed, before the Dining Car runs out of food. Then I'll go over it with you in detail. Now get me my cream-colored teddy in the second drawer."

Beau looked for it, but there were too many silk teddies.

"The other one," Sarah said, while combing out her hair.

"Which one?"

"That one there," she said as she disrobed, took the teddy, and wiggled it down her slim bare body. "My dinner dress, please." Beau handed it to her. She slipped it on. "How do I look?"

"Well…the back is bunched up a bit over there, ma'am."

"Then give it a gentle tug, but do not tear the delicate fabric."

He felt the softness of her shoulders as he gently pulled out her dress.

"…How is it now, Beau?"

He stood back. "Much better, ma'am."

"Good," Sarah said. "Now my evening shoes."

Beau reached into the bottom drawer of her trunk and showed her a pair of T-straps. She took them and said, "My garters and stockings are in the next drawer."

"Ain't you supposed to put 'em on first before your dress?"

Sarah said, "I was in such a rush, I forgot."

He handed her the garters and stockings, but she wouldn't take them. "They don't match. I want the other ones over there."

"There's a lot of 'em, ma'am."

Sarah took what she wanted out of the trunk and handed them to him. "Now, you can give them to me," which he did. She then gently lifted up her dress, sat down, and pulled her stockings over each leg and attached them to her garters.

"How do you know which one is left or right, ma'am?"

She looked up at Beau, not sure what he meant.

"Your stockings, ma'am."

"Doesn't your wife wear stockings?"

"Well, she's a farm girl."

"It doesn't make a difference," Sarah said, standing up straightening out her dress. "How do I look, now?"

"I think you'll do fine, ma'am."

"Good. I'm already for supper. How about you?"

"I'm wearin' what I came with," Beau said, pointing to the evening newspaper. "You didn't finish what you was sayin' about that letter."

"Mr. Benchley came up with the idea of putting it in all the newspapers."

There was a knock on the door.

"Must be that steward again," Sarah said. "Tell him I don't want anything."

"How do you say that in German?"

Sarah said, "'Die Dame braucht nichts' should work."

Beau opened the door and said in English, "See you made it aboard, sir."

"That I did," said Mr. Benchley, stepping into the compartment.

Sarah looked over her shoulder and said, "Glad you could make it on such short notice, Bob."

"I got your note just as you left," Mr. Benchley said. "But all I could find was a coach seat and then I had to wait in line to shave in the men's room. But I'm ready for supper. How about you?"

"More than ready," Sarah said, reaching for the evening paper, "and I've got something to show you."

"Oh, I've already seen it," Mr. Benchley said, showing her his newspaper.

"I suppose certain people are going to have a fit now."

"That was the whole idea of putting it in the newspapers." Mr. Benchley said, "Now, let's head over to the Dining Car before all the schnitzel is gone."

Three cars later they were seated at a four top. Sarah opened the newspaper and translated the published letter into English, while they waited for first course.

Dear Emil,

I trust all is well with you. It seems that another democratic republic, this time Weimar Germany, has allowed men of small aptitude and limited imagination to be set free from the kennel. No doubt that each one of us, in the legal sense, should be treated fairly in matters that are not affected by intelligence, but no sane person would presume everyone to be equal by decree of law, if by nature he is an idiot, halfwit, or nigger. Men should be given tests and those who fail them, or come up short, should be the shoemakers, the street cleaners, and the workers who take orders and *not* give them. Only those who excel should be given the opportunity to reach their fullest potential and not be brutalized and suppressed by fools with limited imagination. The negro need not be given any test for he as an idiot. The Jew, the Chinaman, the Hindu, and the Slav are sub-human. And that brings up the matter of Jesus, who was a Jew, and was possibly the Jew's slyest form of subversion, which is why a new order must be consolidated as soon as possible. Once this little problem is out of the way, we must never again be divided by doubt nor petty notions of the heart. To put it simply, I agree that the scriptures lay bare the path for the lordship of Jesus Christ, but only with a new leader as savior. One who will lead not by moralizing, but by finalizing. Those who dare to resist shall face trial by combat.

Concerning the movement: Thank you, but I cannot lead it as I don't speak German. Major Coors, with his pipsqueak voice, must be removed. I know how hard it will be but listening to him is like listening to my Aunt Lucy. He can also forget that he comes from the gentlemen class. Now, my cousin Egon could lead us, but then it is difficult for a man who has spent his life giving orders behind a desk to then stand on a podium and do the same without his accountant nearby. What Egon doesn't understand is that simple men measure a man by the amount of force that he's willing to use, not the brandy that he has in his decanter, and that is why the Austrian has had some success. We can easily learn from an idiot like him, as it is harder for an idiot to learn from us, but if we allow fear and cowardice to guide us then we are doomed, for courage will always be out of reach.

You will find the letter of release attached. Be wise and make haste, as you already know what to do.

Sincerely,
Ellis Remley

Sarah looked up from the newspaper and said, "I was married to this toad."

Mr. Benchley said, "I hope you told him that while taking down the letter."

"Actually, I told him that the letter was too long and that he needed to cut out everything between Dear and Sincerely."

Beau said, "So, Hugenberg does have the letter of release."

"No…I forgot to send it along."

Mr. Benchley said to Sarah, "I'm sure you did," and then to Beau, "By the way, the *Pegasus* is no longer in port."

"When did you find this out?"

Mr. Benchley said, "I got a call from Brayton Hills on my way out of the hotel."

A passenger then entered the Dining Car with a long scar and a disfigured face. Sarah leaned into Beau, "I think we found our man……"

42

The Red Castle

The guard turned the key and opened the jail cell's heavy iron door. A low-grade inspector stepped inside and said to Al, "Come with me."

Al was brought to the political division. Once inside Inspector Degler's office, he was offered a chair and handed a morning newspaper, *Berliner Morgen-Zietung*, where Ellis Remley's letter to Emil Hugenberg had been reprinted on the front page. Al looked it over and said, "I suppose you think that I had something to do with this."

The inspector said, "One thing for sure is that Sarah Remley has the letter of release," the inspector said, "and she was here the other night swearing that she knew nothing about it and convincingly so."

"You have proof or is this another one of your conjectures?"

"I know that she leaked the letter to all the newspapers."

"Did she call you up and tell you that?"

"She didn't have to," said the inspector. "

Al said, "Mrs. Remley's free to do what she wants or does Germany have laws against that?"

"Not yet…and what was that black American, LaHood, doing on the *Pegasus* the other night?"

"You'd have to ask him," Al said. "I wasn't there."

"I'm asking *you*, because we now can't find him."

"I wouldn't know," Al said.

"You don't seem to know anything."

Al said, "It's hard to know anything stuck in a jail cell."

"Well, if you're trying to make a deal with me, I'm listening."

"I'm not trying to do anything," Al said. "And what's been the government's reaction to this letter, now that it's out?"

"What you'd expect."

"Which is?"

The inspector said, "I've been given the power to go after Coors and his paramilitary group in a way that I hadn't had before."

"And what way is that?"

"What's more interesting at the moment," Inspector Degler said, "is that you're not curious about what happened to that ship?"

"Make me curious," Al said, as he once again looked over the letter that was printed in the *Berliner Morgen-Zeitung*.

Inspector Degler took the newspaper away from him and said, "It was attacked. All the sailors on board are dead. But unfortunately for these pirates there's nowhere the *Pegasus* can sail. Germany is basically landlocked. And the English have been notified and their navy is checking every ship heading out of Hamburg."

"Thanks for telling me," Al said.

"Unless there's another ship at sea where the munitions are to be transferred."

"And what ship would that be?"

"You tell me, Herr Nachman."

"I have no idea."

"Where is Major von Coors sailing the *Pegasus*?"

"You're asking me…?"

"Herr Nachman, it wouldn't surprise me if you had made a deal with von Coors or Hugenberg that, for a flat fee, you'd transfer the arms to another ship of your own."

"I don't own any ships," Al said.

"But Addison Prevette does, and if he wants his little girl back, he'd better play along because Magnus von Coors sent word to Addison

Prevette in New York that neither his ship nor his daughter would be returned unless a round sum of two million dollars was deposited into a certain Swiss bank."

"…When was she kidnapped?"

"What matters," said the inspector, "is that you tell Addison Prevette not to make any monetary concessions to von Coors until we find the *Pegasus* and the munitions on board."

"Well, I have bad news for you, Inspector: Addison Prevette isn't stupid."

"I never said that he was. Just give him a deadline of this coming Sunday at midnight—for the sake of the republic."

Al said, "You're asking me to tell Addison Prevette to risk his child's life on the fat chance that you might get lucky finding a ship?"

"Yes," the inspector said.

"What if the munitions aren't on board?"

"Then your boss has got another problem."

"What's that?"

"The girl will probably die anyway."

"Which is the same problem," Al said.

"In that it has the same ending, but then you're dealing with a politically motivated kidnapping. These paramilitary groups like making a point and they prefer using death, and they're not afraid to, since nearly all the judges, certainly in Bavaria, are more than sympathetic to their cause."

"You know where the girl is being held?"

"I might," Inspector Degler said, "but any foolish move on our part and the girl will surely die, and the other one as well."

"Which other one?"

"Rachel Pschorr," the inspector said.

"Von Coors has both of them?"

"So, then you know her real name."

"She has many names and for good reason," Al said, "but I'll send a wire to Addison Prevette, but only if you tell me where the girls are being held."

"Can't do that."

"You don't tell me where they are, Inspector Degler, then I'm out of this. And if you try to send him a wire using my name, it won't work."

"You can't rescue her on her own, so get that out of your head. The future of this democracy is what's at stake, not the girl, unless you want a little shit like von Coors running Germany and that could easily happen."

"He's not the only little shit out there."

"That's true," the inspector said.

"Where are the girls being held?"

"Herr Nachman, there's nothing that you alone can do."

"I wouldn't be so sure of that."

Inspector Degler said, "Send a wire to Addison Prevette that he doesn't lift a finger to get his child until I give him the okay, or you go back to jail. Von Coors wants that ransom money, because if he does lose the shipment, he'll have funds to secure more arms."

"And what if you can't find the ship by then?"

The inspector returned Al's personal items and said, "We'll worry about that then."

Al gathered his things and said, "I'll see what I can do……"

43

The Dining Car

The man with the scarred face enjoyed the discomfort that he gave the other diners. Half of his mouth was useless as it had been shattered by the fragments of one of nearly two million artillery shells that the allies had fired at the German lines in the first Battle of the Somme. He was told that he was lucky to have come out alive, as if that were supposed to have made him feel any better. He lifted his soup spoon and angled it to the side of his mouth as he couldn't rest it squarely on his crushed lips. The hot liquid bled back into the soup bowl. Sarah watched this as she took her lipstick from her purse and let it fall to the floor, so that it would roll to his table. The scarred man reached over and handed her the tube. Sarah thanked him in German. He said, "A pleasure to help a lady as beautiful as you." She let their eyes meet for a moment, just long enough to be friendly. Then she went back to her pot roast and cabbage. When the man with the scarred face finished his supper, he left the dining room car alone. Beau got up and said, "I'm gonna take a little walk."

Sarah said, "Mr. Benchley and I will be in the Club Car for an after- dinner drink. I have a feeling that he'll end up there."

Beau said, "Then so will I."

Beau left the Dining Car and followed the man with the scar to Compartment 4 in the third car. Beau then headed to where the stewards were posted at the end of the train car, thinking that they would have a passenger list up on the wall, but there wasn't one. He tried several other cars and soon enough realized that it operated differently than a Pullman train. Beau went back to his car to get his horn, maybe make some friends in the Club Car, see what he could learn about Sigmaringen. When he opened the compartment door, he said, "Sorry, ma'am. Thought you was in the Club Car."

"Where are you going, Beau?"

"I'll wait till you get done changin', ma'am."

"No, I need you here. The Dining Car waiter dripped coffee on my dress."

"…Seems you get a lot of stains, ma'am."

"What're you trying to say, Beau?"

"Not a thing, ma'am."

Sarah handed him her dress and then sat down on the plush bench couch in her teddy. She lit up and waited for him to finish.

Beau said, "I followed the man with the scar to Car 3, Compartment 4."

"Good. I think I've got a plan."

"What's that?"

Sarah said, "I'll let you know when the time is ready…Now, I bet you were the best porter on the train back home."

"I was First Porter on the 20th Century Limited, ma'am."

"Probably cleaned a lot of dresses and men's' suits, too."

Beau looked up for a second. "Well, you know how it is on a train, everythin' shakin'."

Sarah reached for an ashtray and balanced it on her bare knee.

Beau said, "Might fall off like that."

Sarah nudged the ashtray higher up her bare thigh. "You want the upper or lower berth?"

"…Ma'am?"

"You want to sleep upper or lower?"

"Well, whichever is more convenient for you," Beau said, as he worked on the coffee spot with a damp cloth.

"I think the upper birth is more fun," Sarah said, crossing her legs and rubbing a sudden itch.

"Kids always like to sleep up there," Beau said.

"I'm a kid."

Beau kept his eyes on her dress. "What's that, ma'am?"

"It's true. I'm just a kid. I mean, I'm so tired of playing the adult. Why can't we just be kids when we want without being shamed for something that we all want to do anyway?"

"I think this stain is almost out," Beau said holding up her dress.

"Good. Now do my teddy."

"Your teddy…?"

"The coffee seeped right through and gave it a terrible stain." Sarah slipped off her teddy and tossed it over to Beau. All she had on, now, were her stockings, garters, and t-straps."

"Could get you a blanket, iffen you cold, ma'am."

"I'll let you know if I'm cold." She flicked an ash. "I suppose there was a masseuse on your train as well, since it's posh."

"A what…?"

"A masseuse. You know," Sarah said, wiggling her fingers.

"Actually, I don't know."

"Well, you should. I'm so stiff, I can't even touch my toes. It's these German beds. Next time I'm going to bring my own." Sarah bent all the way over with her arms spread out. "They call this the Swan."

Beau looked up. "…The what?"

"The Swan, even though I'm stiff as an ironing board." Sarah then pretended that she was in flight. "I wanted to be a dancer, a serious one, like Anna Pavlova, but that was out of the question."

"What was?"

"Dancing."

"Dancin'…?"

"Yes, but then a woman of my class doesn't dance professionally unless she wants to lose her position in society. You're a servant. You should know that."

"Well, actually," Beau said, "I got this new job, as I told you and—"

"You still should know."

"Know what, ma'am?"

"You've served ladies before."

"None of them was dancin' ladies."

"I would hope not," Sarah said.

"Somethin' wrong with dancin', ma'am?"

"Our people don't *do* certain, things."

"They don't dance?"

"Certainly not on a stage," Sarah said, surprised at his ignorance. "I wouldn't want people to think that I'm loose."

He looked up from the teddy. "Is that what *loose* is?"

"Well," Sarah said, "that's how a girl gets started. Everyone knows that. I only dance at a ball or a proper evening club."

"Oh," Beau said. "I didn't know that."

"Now you do…Do you want to give it a try?"

"Uhh, give what a try, ma'am?"

Sarah opened her hands and wiggled her fingers.

Beau held up the empty glass of soda water and said, "Looks like this here spot needs more than a little soda water."

"Beau…"

"Yes, ma'am?"

"I'd rather have a spot on my teddy then a stiff neck."

There was a knock on the door. Sarah responded to it in a loud but firm voice, "Ich bin gerade beschäftigt!" The person on the other side answered in English. Sarah slipped on her robe and opened the door.

Mr. Benchley was surprised to see her robed and with Beau in the room. He said to her, "I just saw someone in the Club Car with a scar down his face, but—"

"What?"

"He's not the person whom we saw in the Dining Car."

Sarah said, "Go back to the Club Car and don't lose sight of him."

"What about you?"

"Well, I've got to get dressed first……"

44

Schlackwurst

The taper candle flickered shadows onto Zola. She was curled up in the corner against the stone wall of the tower. Her eyes were dark and weary. "Where's my coat? I want my coat and my dress."

The Keeper of Keys removed the chamber pot and set a plate with dried cured sausage and black bread on the floor beside to her.

"Don't you have something warm to eat?"

"Black bread is good for you," he said.

"I'm *freezing*," Zola said. "*Get* me my clothing. I won't run away. I promise. I can barely get to the door."

"I'm not allowed to do that."

She pushed away the dry sausage. "I *want* my coat."

"Sausage is good for you."

"*What* have I done to you people? Why are you treating me this way? I want my coat. I *want* my coat."

"Sausage is good for you."

"I have money," Zola said. "I'll give you 10,000 American dollars once I get to Berlin."

The Keeper of Keys said, "I'll get you some more butter. Butter is good for you."

"You might as well get me a newspaper to eat."

"I can get you a newspaper, but it's old."

"I don't want to eat a newspaper. I'm *freezing*. How do I get it through your head that I'm cold?"

The Keeper of Keys closed the ancient door behind him and disappeared into the castle.

45

Big Sissy

The Ford-Werke sedan drove up the steep narrow hill to the castle. It stopped just short of the portcullis and blinked its headlights. Heinz, the driver, said to Fritz in the passenger seat, "You sure we lost the car that was following us?"

"There wasn't any car following us."

Heinz said, "I know when a car is following me. I drove a party leader through Mindelheim once and someone from the Reichsbanner Schwarz-Rot-Gold party tried to cut us off, but I was too good for those sissies."

"Karl Mayr is no sissy."

Heinz said to Fritz, "You only like him because he was an officer in the war."

"He was a fine officer."

"He supports the faggot parliamentary system," Heinz said.

"Yeah, but he's seen war and a man who's seen war is to be respected."

The portcullis opened.

Heinz drove through and said, "He's still a big sissy."

Fritz pointed to the backseat and said, "Just keep your hands off the girls, for now."

Shelby and Ilse were brought into the castle and taken to the Crown Prince's chamber where a desk, flanked by wooden benches on the walls, faced the door. The DNF, or Die Deutsche Nationale Freiheitspartei, flag was mounted behind it. It was red and centered with a golden eagle that clenched an Iron Cross in one claw, and a flaming torch in the other. The only window faced the Danube River and the Black Forest beyond. A party member sitting on one of the benches was slowly eating an apple the way a worm does. Otto Zumbach said to Fritz in the doorway, "Which one of them is the American?"

Heinz said, "I think they both are."

Otto Zumbach said, "I'm talking to Fritz."

Fritz said, "They're both Americans."

Otto Zumbach said, "Did you have any problems on the way?"

"Everything went smoothly," Fritz said.

"There were a bunch of sissies following us," Heinz said.

Fritz said, "No one was following us."

Otto Zumbach said, "Which one is the Jewess?"

Fritz pointed to Ilse.

The Keeper of Keys then entered the chamber.

Otto Zumbach said to him, "What do you want?"

"Well, sir," the Keeper of Keys said, "she wants to read a newspaper."

"Who wants to read a newspaper?"

The Keeper of Keys pointed to the tower and then glanced at Shelby and Rachel who were still gagged and bound.

"Tell her she can't," Otto Zumbach said. "And move her from the tower. I don't want them with her."

"Where should I put her?" the Keeper of Keys said, his eye still on the girls.

"You're supposed to be the expert on this castle," Otto Zumbach said.

The Keeper of Keys shuffled out of the chamber. He stopped and said, "She also wants her clothing."

"Maybe she wants spaghetti, too," Otto Zumbach said.

"She didn't tell me that."

"That's because you're stupid."

The Keeper of Keys said, "You shouldn't talk to me like that."

"Are you telling me what to do?"

"No," said the Keeper of Keys, "I just want to be respected."

"Then why tell me everything that she wants? Are you working for her?"

"No, sir."

"Did she promise you money?"

"I don't think so."

"You don't think so…?"

"No."

"How about sex?"

"No," the Keeper of Keys said, as he shuffled his way out of the chamber.

"Did I tell you to go?"

The Keeper of Keys stopped at the edge of the doorway. "…No."

"So, then, where the hell are you going?"

The Keeper of Keys stood there looking down at the floor.

Otto Zumbach pointed to Ilse and said to the man eating the apple, "Is that the girl you saw at that cabaret in Berlin."

"Yes," Heinz said.

"Was I talking to you?"

"No."

The man sitting on the bench eating the apple said, "That's Ilse Dietrich."

"Good," Otto Zumbach said. "And what about the other girl?"

"She's the rich one."

"Good…"

46

Wolfie

S arah Remley entered the Club Car and said to Mr. Benchley in English, "I want you to meet Wolfrik Ritter von Feffenhausen. Otherwise known as Wolfie—he speaks no English."

Mr. Benchley tried to smile, but it was sabotaged by rivalry. "And just how did you find *Mr.* Wolfie?"

"I ran into him on my way here."

"Yes, but how?"

Sarah said, "Compartment 4, third car." She then turned to Wolfie and said in German, "Meet my brother, Bob," and then to Mr. Benchley in English, "He's invited me to his compartment for a drink."

"I thought you were just there."

"I was, Bob, but first I thought I'd stop by, if you know what I mean."

"Well, tell him you can't go."

"Oh, I'm going—he's the one we've been looking for."

Mr. Benchley said, "Then I'm coming along."

Sarah touched his shoulder and said, "Bob, this is business, not love," and kissed him on the cheek. She and Wolfie took off.

Wolfrik Ritter von Feffenhausen shut the door to his compartment and offered Sarah some whiskey and a Walküre cigarette.

"My favorite brand," Sarah lied.

They lit up, clinked glasses, and sat down on the bench couch.

"I hope I don't come across as rude, Wolfie, but I just have to know what happened to your face?"

"The war."

"Yes, but what happened?"

"An artillery shell," Wolfie said as he opened up his arms to mimic an explosion.

"I'm surprised it didn't kill you."

"It just about did."

Sarah said, "I saw someone else on the train with a scar just like yours. I suppose an awful a lot of people went through the same horrible experience."

"More than you can imagine," he said, as she gently moved his hand from her thigh. She then touched his face and exerted some pressure with her fingers. He flinched.

"Oh, I'm sorry. Did I hurt you?"

"Yes, it's a little sensitive," he said, still absorbing the pain.

"Were you and that other man in the same regiment?"

"What other man?"

"The one on the train with the scar like yours."

"No, but it turns out that he's a Jew," Wolfie said.

"Really? You mean there were Jews serving in the German army?"

"Too many as far as I'm concerned," Wolfie said.

"Why that's terrible," she said, as she reached into her clutch bag and showed him the enamel pin that she had taken off her cousin's desk.

Wolfie took it from her. "Where did you get this?"

"I'm a member," Sarah lied.

"But you're an American."

"My family is German."

"Really? Well, I'm not surprised with your good looks."

"Are you a member?"

"No," Wolfie said, "I'm with the Deutsche Nationale Freiheitsparteie,"

"Something wrong with the Nazis?"

"Their core beliefs, I agree with," Wolfie said. "It's their leader whom I don't like."

"You mean that Austrian corporal?"

"Yes. He's a weasel," Wolfie said, staring into her eyes.

Sarah gently pushed his other hand away. "Well, something has to be done, if he's a weasel. Don't you think?"

"Oh, something will be done," Wolfie said.

"Correct me if I'm wrong, but isn't a man named von Coors the leader of the DNF?"

"You seem to know a lot for an American."

Sarah said, "You must know him well."

"You could say so."

"Is he anything like the Austrian?"

Wolfie said, "They have big ideas."

"Is that good?"

"I have ideas myself," Wolfie said.

"Are you frustrated that no one listens to you?"

"I wouldn't say that."

"Well, I want to be with the man who's the boss of the party."

"Don't you worry your little head off," Wolfie said, touching her bottom. "I'll be the boss of the party one day, and your boss once we get married."

"You think we should do that?"

"Absolutely," Wolfie said.

"Would I be wrong to think that's why fate has put us together?"

"No doubt," Wolfie said, creeping his hand under her dress.

"But what if we should never meet again?" Sarah said, pushing back his hand.

"Why would you say that?"

"What if this is all a dream?"

"I'll take you to the castle and hide you from anyone who wants to hurt you," Wolfie said.

"…You have a castle?"

"I have many things for you."

"Where is this castle?"

"By a lovely river," Wolfie said.

"Is this castle yours?"

"Why don't you wait and see?"

"Where is it?"

"Let it be a surprise," Wolfie said.

"Are you a prince?"

"I'm more than that," Wolfie said.

"Well, do I just knock on the front door?"

"You're funny."

"How many times should I knock?"

"You silly girl." He tried to kiss her with his stubbly lips. She turned away.

"Are you going there now?"

"You could say."

"For a vacation?"

"Exactly," Wolfie said, his hand back under her dress.

Again, she pushed it away. "I suppose the castle is where you hide *all* your girls."

"I would never do such a thing," Wolfie said.

"I bet the ones you don't like you put in the tower."

"They never get in the castle," Wolfie said, kissing her shoulder and then sweeping his fingers through her lovely hair.

"Wolfie, I'm very serious. I want to be your only girl. Not some pickup."

"I wouldn't have it any other way," he lied.

"Well, I'm a good girl. You'll have to marry me first."

"I'll marry you tomorrow," he said.

There was a knock on the door.

Wolfie raised his voice and said, "You've got the wrong compartment."

"I'm the train conductor, sir, and a gentleman is looking for his wife. He told me your name. That's why I'm here."

Wolfie said to Sarah, "I *thought* he was your brother."

"So, did I," she said, getting up, straightening out her dress, looking for a mirror to fix her hair.

Wolfie reluctantly opened the compartment door out of respect to the conductor.

Mr. Benchley looked inside and immediately scented mischief. Beau was just behind him.

Sarah said to Wolfie in German, "Let me have a word with them."

Wolfie said, "Just get rid of them."

"I'll do my best without being rude."

She then said to Mr. Benchley in English. "He's our man and the girls are in the castle."

"Do you have proof?"

"Bob, what we don't have is time."

Wolfie interrupted, "What's his problem?"

Sarah said to him, "Just give me minute."

Wolfie said, "Tell them to get lost."

"That's exactly what I'm doing but, as a lady, I must be discreet. I'm sure you can understand that."

Sarah then said to Beau and Mr. Benchley in English, "This is what we're going to do."

Beau said, "I don't like the way he's looking at me."

Sarah said, "Soon he won't be looking at anyone."

"What do you mean by that?" said Mr. Benchley

"We're going to throw him off the train," Sarah said.

Benchley looked at the carriage doors and said to her, "You're crazy."

Sarah said to Beau, "You've worked on the railroad. How much of a chance does he have of surviving if we push him out?"

"Well, that all depends," Beau said.

"On what?"

"Where it happens. But there's a viaduct we got to crossover soon. In fact, there's two on the way."

"How do you know that?"

"I always study a train route before it departs. It's in my travel guide."

"How high is this viaduct?" Sarah said.

"High enough, I would imagine."

"When will we get to it?"

"I'm guessin' a quarter of an hour or so."

Wolfie again interrupted Sarah. "*Will* you get rid of them already."

"They're just about to go," Sarah said, as she touched Wolfie in a reassuring way. Then she said to Mr. Benchley now that the conductor had gone. "Hit him as hard as you can in his face. He'll fall right over."

Mr. Benchley wasn't too sure about that.

Sarah said to him, "You heard me."

"And if he doesn't fall over?"

Sarah said, "I touched his face before, and he flinched as if I'd hit him with a baseball bat. Then we'll tie him up."

"With what?"

"Excuse me," Beau interrupted, "but y'all don't wanna tie him up."

"Why not?" Sarah said.

"Because y'all want it to look like suicide. Him all tied up it gonna look like murder—because that's what it is."

Mr. Benchley said to Sarah, "Did you hear what Beau just said?"

"Suicide is what I heard."

Mr. Benchley said, "This is crazy."

Sarah turned to Beau, "I hope you haven't forgotten the blood that was all over Rachel's apartment."

"I haven't," Beau said feeling the train ascend. "And it seems the first of the viaducts is here sooner than I had thought."

Wolfie said to Sarah in German, "I've had enough of this nonsense. Get them out of here, or I'll throw them out."

She said to him, "If they think I'm in trouble, they won't go. So please, be patient. It'll take just a another second." She then said to Mr. Benchley and Beau, "The hell are you two waiting for?"

Mr. Benchley said, "This is nuts."

Sarah said, "Then leave."

Mr. Benchley said, "I suppose you're going to punch him all by your little self."

"Unlike you, Mr. Snowflake, I'm going to confront evil."

Mr. Benchley said, "There are other ways of confronting evil."

"And there are too many ways of avoiding it."

"I'm not avoiding anything," said Mr. Benchley. "I'm trying not to make things worse."

"You are making things worse by doing nothing. The people who kidnapped the girls are no doubt waiting for him. So, we're going to beat them at their own game."

"What game is that?"

Sarah said to Mr. Benchley, "We're going to take one of their pieces off the board, something they don't expect."

Mr. Benchley said, "It's still crazy."

"Then leave. Beau and I will do it."

Before Beau could say a word, Wolfie pushed Sarah to the side and said, "I'm getting them out of here right now." He made the mistake of strong-arming Mr. Benchley in way that turns a gentle soul into a beast. Mr. Benchley not only hit him square in the face, but then kicked him there for good measure. Mr. Benchley then opened the carriage doors. The winter air rushed in. He grabbed the German and heaved him into the darkness of the valley as the train rushed by. Beau broke the silence and said, "Should they find him, and sooner or later they will, the police gonna speak to the conductor of this train concernin' who was on it to narrow down the suspects."

"They won't find anyone," Sarah said. "It's too heavily wooded here."

"They gonna find him, ma'am."

"We'll be out of Germany by then," Sarah assured him.

"And just how do you know that?"

Mr. Benchley said, "She doesn't…"

47

Along the Watchtower

The Keeper of Keys did not like these political men who did not belong to the castle. They did not respect tradition. They did not respect him. Thinking of them only made him angrier as he climbed the steep stairway to the parapet walk that led to where he had hidden Zola's winter coat, gloves, cloche, dress, shoes, and handbag in a secret alcove. He bundled them into his arms and went across the parapet to the southern tower where he placed her things beside her for when she'd wake, but it was never to happen. He knew it as soon as he touched her.

48

Power

The Keeper of Keys did not sit down when he returned to his rooms. He stood by the window and looked out into the endless Schwarzwald and imagined what freedom was like on the other side. Elke came in and said, "Your supper is ready."

The Keeper of Keys turned away from the window and said "…The girl is dead."

"The one in the tower?"

"…They wouldn't let me help her."

"You were afraid."

"…I'm always afraid."

Elke came to him and said, "That's because you don't understand those who want power."

"What don't I understand?"

"If you want power for the sake of power, you'll always live a life of tragedy, because to keep it you must be cruel……"

49

Deutsche Haus

The midnight sleeper arrived in Sigmaringen with a trail of smoke that knitted gray lazy clouds into the sky. Passengers disembarked with children, hand luggage, tied boxes, and a wind that blew their hats off. Beau, Sarah, and Mr. Benchley got off the train and took a livery car to the Deutsches Haus on Fürst Wilhelmstraße, just down the hill from the castle.

On their way up to their rooms, Sarah said to Mr. Benchley, "The concierge told me that there isn't place to develop and print film here, so since you're good at sketching all you'll have to do is play the part of the tourist while keeping an eye on who goes in and out of the castle."

"You're lucky I don't mind taking orders from a woman."

"You're lucky I don't mind giving them," Sarah said with a smile, and then to Beau, "Are you sure you have to go to that Fastnacht committee now?"

"That's what Ziggy said I should do soon as I arrive."

"Is she already in town?"

"At her folk's house," Beau said.

"Then come back here as soon as you're done," Sarah said, entering her room—Beau thinking maybe Al should've hired Sarah instead.

Mr. Benchley said to her, "I'll grab my sketchpad and head over to the castle now."

"Good," Sarah said. "We'll see you shortly……"

50

Khartoum

Emil Hugenberg's study reeked of unscrubbed Victorian odors and dried Ottoman dung. It was said that he hadn't opened a window since the Wahehe Rebellion. Al Nachman would have agreed as he took the old brown leather chair that Gordon had once sat in and then slowly sank into Khartoum. "Have you read the papers today, Herr Hugenberg?"

"I have."

"Good, because now the whole country knows what you and the DNF are up to."

"It's all a lie."

Al said, "I thought you changed after having read Bloch's *The Future of War*."

"I may have, but the past hasn't. Now, this is the situation as it stands. Prevette's daughter will die unless there is a transfer of two million dollars to this account." Emil Hugenberg handed Al a piece of paper.

"…Von Coors' account?"

"It's irrelevant."

Al said, "I want to hear her voice before anything is done."

"I have nothing to do with the girl's release. I'm just passing on what I've been told, so do not treat me like a villain when I'm only trying to help you."

Al said, "There's no way we can proceed without my knowing that the girl is alive."

"I can assure you that she is."

"You can assure me all you want," Al said, "but Addison Prevette needs proof that his daughter is not dead, because he's not about to send anything without hearing her voice."

"That would be hard since he's not in Germany. Or is he, Herr Nachman?"

"I want to hear her voice," Al said.

"I don't think you understand. The Major gets the money by the deadline, or she will die."

Al leaned over and said, "You get the girl on the phone right now, otherwise you're in for something worse."

"You're bullying me, Mr. Nachman. I find it pathetic if not ungentlemanly, as I'm merely passing on information but, having said that, how much do you want? Because it's obvious that's why you're here."

"I don't want anything."

"You have the keys to the cargo hold of the *Pegasus*."

"I want to hear the girl's voice," Al said.

"I'll give you $10,000 and no one will know."

"I want to hear the girl's voice."

"You going to turn down $30,000?"

"So now it's $30,000?"

"From a generous man whom you enjoy insulting."

"Then I'll to have to do something you won't like," Al said.

"What?"

"Bring the Political Division into this."

"Oh, I can buy Inspector Degler anytime I want."

"Maybe on a misdemeanor charge," Al said, "but his country is not for sale."

"Mr. Nachman, we're talking about a boat not a country."

Al got up and walked over to the window that faced the street. "Take a look outside."

Emil Hugenberg rose from his chair and looked outside. He saw Inspector Degler looking right up at him from the street.

Al said, "Inspector Degler would love to get his hands on you and those financial documents. But all you have to do is get the girl on the telephone so I can hear her voice, otherwise you'll hang."

"Mr. Nachman, we don't hang people here."

"Oh, I forgot. You chop their heads off."

Emil Hugenberg stepped away from the window and said, "…Are you really a Jew?"

The anger in Al's eyes put meaning into the words, "I'm the son of a bitch who'll kill you, if you don't get her on the line."

"You won't get away with killing me."

"And you won't be alive to find out." Al forced Emil Hugenberg's hand onto the telephone. The operator came through and requested a connection.

Emil Hugenberg said, "Sigmaringen……"

51

The Vigil

The Keeper of Keys, now on his way back from the hardware store with a new set of keys, made his way up the steep path to the castle. He noticed a stranger sketching something on a pad. Curious, the Keeper of Keys looked over the stranger's shoulder. He did not like what he saw, and he told Mr. Benchley in so many words that the angles were different once you got further away from the castle, but Mr. Benchley did not understand him. So, Mr. Benchley flipped the pages over for a clean sheet of paper to appease the chattering man, and as he did the Keeper of Keys stopped him at the sketch of Shelby and Ilse that Mr. Benchley had drawn at the Café Josty, back in Berlin. The Keeper of Keys pointed up to the castle and then back to the sketchbook. Mr. Benchley now understood the man.

The Keeper of Keys lead him through the portcullis and into the bailey where a man from the DNF was loitering. He did not bother Mr. Benchley as he was dressed like a gentleman, but he did not take his eyes off him, either. The Keeper of Keys did not care. He was no longer afraid of these wicked men. Mr. Benchley and the Keeper of Keys entered the castle and continued on through several long stone passageways until they reached a magnificent grand ballroom filled with immense paintings, chandeliers, and a gilded ceiling. From there they went through another corridor that led all the way up to the tower door. When the door was opened, Shelby and Ilse were stunned to see Mr. Benchley.

"…How did you find us?" Shelby said.

Mr. Benchley said, "This man over here."

"Yes," Shelby said, "but how did know that we were in Sigmaringen?"

Mr. Benchley said, "You can thank Beau and Mrs. Remley for that."

"Yes, but *how*?"

"A box of matches found in Ilse's apartment," Mr. Benchley said. "Now, how long have you two been here?"

"Long enough," Shelby said. "Is Beau here as well?"

"Yes, and so is Mrs. Remley."

The Keeper of Keys interrupted them and spoke to Shelby. She then said to Mr. Benchley, "He's telling me that something will soon happen."

"What?"

"I don't know, but he talks about the dead."

"Ask him what happened to Zola."

"I already have," Shelby said, "but he says that he knows nothing."

The Keeper of Keys interrupted them and said in German, "And I'm not an idiot like the men downstairs think, but when the third Norn comes, we shall all be free, and they shall all die."

Shelby said to Mr. Benchley, "He's now talking about the Norns."

"The what…?"

Ilse said to Mr. Benchley, "The legend of the Norns."

"What's that all about?"

Ilse said, "Nordic mythology. You see, he thinks that Shelby and I are two of the three Norns and that he has to protect us until the third one arrives." She then said to the Keeper of Keys, "The third Norn has arrived. She is in town. You may begin the vigil."

The Keeper of Keys said to the girls, "Good. Come with me. I will hide you in the castle where they can't find you."

Shelby said to him, "Get us out of the castle, we don't want to stay here a second longer."

"I can't risk that," the Keeper of Keys said. "There is a big meeting tonight. Men coming from out of town, and very shortly guards will be posted everywhere—some more have just arrived—and they will see you, but I can take your friend out of the castle."

Shelby said, "If you can take him out, you can take us out."

The Keeper of Keys said, "You will never make it once they see you."

"Isn't there another way out of this dungeon?" Shelby said.

"Nowhere that they can't see you. But only I know every room in the castle and they will never find where I hide you. Now come......."

52

Banana Dancer

The Ford-Werke Sedan entered a dirt road that led to a vintage Bavarian country house made of wood and mortar just outside the town of Sigmaringen. Otto Zumbach stepped out of the sedan with fresh flowers in hand and rang the mechanical door bell. Frau Coors greeted him, wearing the cook's apron. "Are those for me, Otto?"

"Why yes, Frau Coors. A man with resource can always find spring in winter for a lady as noble as you."

"Otto, you can charm a bird off a tree when you want." She took the flowers and brought her guest in. "My son is having his supper. I'll get something for you, too."

"No, I'm fine, but thank you just the same, Frau Coors."

Once inside the dining room, Otto Zumbach sat down and said to the Major, "Where is everyone?"

"In town preparing for the carnival tonight."

"And the servants?"

"Everyone is gone except for my mother and Ziggy—I told you to stay in the castle."

"I thought I'd stop by; see how you were doing," Otto Zumbach said.

"Where are Fräulein Prevette and Ilse, now?"

"Secured in the castle."

"Was the money sent?"

"…There was a little problem," Otto Zumbach said.

"What do you mean little problem? Didn't you speak to that American clown who works for Addison Prevette?"

"I did, but then he spoke to Hugenberg."

"And…?"

"Americans are funny," Otto Zumbach said.

"They're stupid is what they are."

"We had to let him speak to the girl."

"You what…?"

"Just to let him know that she's alive," Otto Zumbach said. "Then he told me that, as far as her father was concerned, we can keep his daughter because he's sick of her."

"…*Who* said that?"

"Addison Prevette."

"You spoke to him?"

"To the American," Otto Zumbach said.

"He's lying; otherwise, why would he have bothered to talk to her?"

"Magnus, he wanted to see if *we* were lying."

"What about the money?"

"He's not sending the money."

"Then he's not getting her," the Major said.

"You still plan on killing her just to make a point?"

"Yes."

"Magnus, the American said that you should marry her to take her off her father's hands. He's sick of all the trouble that she causes the family."

"If you believe that then you're an idiot," the Major said. "What about the Jewess?"

"Everyone in Berlin is looking for her. Ilse's already missed two shows and word has been leaked that she's been kidnapped and so, in effect, you're no longer negotiating with Addison Prevette but with all of Europe."

"Fuck Europe," said the Major as he slurped his soup.

Otto Zumbach took a newspaper from his coat pocket and showed it to the Major. "This is no longer about some American girl missing, but the biggest star of Europe."

The Major said, "I thought the biggest star in Europe was that nigger banana dancer from America?"

"They're both from America."

"A banana dancer of all things," the Major said. "The fuck's the matter with Americans?"

"Magnus, if Berlin gets Ilse back then we won't have to worry about the police, because no one cares about the other girl."

"Fuck 'em all."

"Magnus…"

"We're keeping both girls."

"Magnus, I think you should reconsider."

"That cunt bitch lied to me."

"Yeah, but—"

"Everyone now thinks that I've been sleeping with a Jewess and have got Jew slime all over me."

"Yeah, but no one can hold that against you if she wasn't telling the truth."

"Otto…you *don't* seem to understand."

"What don't I understand?"

"If I didn't know that she was a Jewess, then how do I know if anyone else is? You *do* understand what I'm saying?"

"Magnus, you were tricked. Jews are very good at that."

"You *miss* the point, Otto. You could be a fucking Jew—*I* could be one."

"Is that what's bothering you?"

"*Yes……*"

53

The Bayou's Howl

The narrow ancient streets of Sigmaringen were lined with medieval fachwerk houses. One of them had a placard declaring *Die Fastnacht-Komitee* on its door. Beau entered and climbed up a spine of narrow, creaky stairs that led to a large room thick with heavy beams and timeworn wooden planks. Costumes with strange wooden masks were mounted everywhere on stands that bore the names of those who had worn them in Fastnachts past. He then approached a small door that had been built when people didn't live long and knocked on it. An elderly woman opened it and said in German, "You must be Beau LaHood. I'm Frau Kleister. I was told that you speak some German, but I will talk to you slowly so that you may understand me and, if not, don't worry; you are very much welcomed here." She showed him inside. The room was filled with needle workers sitting at benches. "Now, I don't mean to be rude, but you're the first black man that I've ever met, let alone seen. My son wrote to me from the front that he had fought against you people and that you had killed many of our boys, but then the war is done with and so is he." One of the needle workers handed Frau Kleister a Fastnacht costume. "This is for you, Beau, and you shall wear it tonight and be one of us. Now, Ziggy told me that you play jazz from New Orleans, where they too have the carnival. I have only heard this music from the children who gather on Saturday nights in the dance hall." A girl, in her late teens, opened the door and walked in. She carried a trumpet case. Frau Kleister said, "This is Henni. She is the girl who loves American music. She is the founder of the Sigmaringen Charleston Dance Club where all the young come to hear her collection of American records. She also plays along with her horn. Now, Henni doesn't speak any English, but you will find her charming nonetheless, and I know you two will get along just fine. Ziggy also mentioned that when you play your saxophone you voice the spirits from the other side, and since I'm nearing that side, I would like to hear what will be greeting me."

Frau Kleister nodded to Henni who took out her trumpet and began to warm up with a few scales before playing *Five Foot Two, Eyes of Blue.* Beau took out his horn but transitioned to *Gut Bucket Blues* and so did Henni. She was playing under and over his riff as if born of the Bayou's howl. When they finished, Frau Kleister said, "That's some greeting I'll be getting…"

54

Under the Spell

Ziggy found her brother on the living room sofa staring into space. "Magnus, get up. I've got your costume for tonight." She leaned over and shook him. "Get up, Magnus. The committee needs to see you in your costume before the parade starts and you know how Frau Kleister is."

"…What's an Episcopalian?"

"The hell do I know," Ziggy said, taking out his Fastnacht costume. "Ilse said she was an Episcopalian."

"Look, Magnus, Frau Kleister needs—"

"What's an Episcopalian?"

"Who cares? Now, get up," Ziggy said, tugging at him.

"I was in love with her."

"You'll find a new girl."

"They escaped," the Major said.

"*Who* escaped?"

"I just got the call."

"Who called?"

"From Otto as soon as he returned to the castle. Ilse and the other girl can't be found."

"Look, Magnus, I don't know what you're talking about, but that's one big castle and easy to get lost in. Now, put this on."

"…Why do stupid people think they're smart?"

"Look, Magnus, we don't have all night."

"I thought she was everything in this world," the Major said, staring into nowhere again.

"Who was?"

"Ilse, who else?"

"How many times have I told you that she's not your type?" Ziggy took out the big head that was part of the costume.

"She not only had mystic beauty," the Major said, "but it was the sound of her voice, the way she moved. I was under that witch's spell."

"Look, Magnus, it's late and it's getting dark." Ziggy tried to get him into his costume. "You'll have trouble leading the parade if this doesn't fit you correctly."

"I guess you didn't know that Ilse was kidnapped."

"I know all about it," Ziggy said. "I just wish that I had thought of it earlier."

"Why…?"

"The publicity is amazing. We're getting flooded with calls from all over Europe, and they better not find her too quickly, because it's the best thing that's ever happened to the cabaret, besides Ilse."

"…I hate berries," the Major said, as Ziggy helped him get into the oversized Dutch style pants that bellowed out.

"Hate 'em or not, just remember not to bend too far over or you're gonna fall and not be able get back up on your own."

The Major stared at the gigantic oversized black head with flashing yellow eyes, gorging mouth, giant orange ears, and little pink hat that was attached to the top of the head. The Major said, "This stupid thing has gotta be ten times bigger than my head."

"That's the idea," Ziggy said, trying to slip it over his ears.

"I want something more dignified."

"*Hold* still. If you want something more dignified, then you'll have to wait until the festival is over."

"What's with the little pink hat?"

"I thought it looked cute," Ziggy said.

"*Cute*? I want something more dignified than *cute*. I'm the one leading the damn parade tonight, *not* cute.

"It's too late," Ziggy said. "I showed your costume to the committee and once it's approved the leader has to wear it." She lifted up his arms so that he could get into the purple coat with gold buttons.

"…There's something I don't understand," the Major said, halfway inside the costume.

"You don't have to understand everything in life."

"You're not hiding something from me, are you?"

"I am *not* hiding anything from you, Magnus. You're just always suspicious. Now hurry up; Frau Kleister is waiting."

"Why does such a terrific person like me always get treated like garbage?"

"…You're asking a big question, Magnus."

"How could someone tell a kidnapper to keep their child? What kind of depraved father is that?"

"Put the other shoe on," Ziggy said.

He looked down at the floor. "These are the ugliest shoes that I've ever seen in my life."

"They're very nice," Ziggy said, helping him put them on.

"If your kid got kidnapped, would you tell them to keep her?"

"I don't know."

"What do you mean you don't know?"

"Maybe they've got a reason," Ziggy said.

"*What* reason?"

"Look Magnus, if you had been kidnapped, Papa would've said the same thing."

"What…"

"*Keep* him……"

55

Fear

The cuckoo bird popped out of its clock in the Deutsches Haus sitting room and loudly cuckooed. Sarah had had enough of sitting around. She got up and went to the front desk to see if Beau had already returned. Instead, she found her cousin Egon von Remmele signing the guest book. She approached him and said, in English, "Well, cousin, long time no see."

Egon looked up from the guestbook.

"Sarah…?"

"Yes, how are you Egon?"

"What on earth are you doing here?"

"I could say that of you. Where were you?"

"Where *was* I?"

"I came to your mansion, and you stuck me with that old Hugenberg."

"Oh, sorry about that," Egon said, "but you hadn't wired us, and we had no idea that you were already here."

"Egon, I wired you from the ship and then notified your household from the Hotel Esplanade as soon as I got to Berlin."

"What about the children?"

"…What about them?"

"You left them in New York?"

"They're with my mother," Sarah said.

"What're you doing in Germany?"

"Vacationing."

"Yes, of course," Egon said. "Well, there's no need for you to be staying at some hotel. You bring your trunks straight to the house when you get back to Berlin. Anna has been in tears about the whole thing."

"Has she?"

"Yes," Egon said, "but why are you here, of all places?"

"I just told you," Sarah said.

"No, I mean Sigmaringen."

"I have an acquaintance who suggested that I come see the festival. And you?"

"Oh, I'm just stopping over for the night," Egon said.

"Why?"

"Well, I have some business that needs to be attended to in Zürich."

"Switzerland?"

"Yes," Egon said.

"Banking?"

"I can assure you, nothing of interest to a woman."

"Then you know nothing of my interests," Sarah said, looking around the lobby. "And where's Anna? On her way over from the train station?"

"Oh no, she's at home with the children. There's a school break coming up and we will all be going to St. Moritz to ski and toboggan. You must join us."

"I shall," Sarah said, aware of the man at the far end of the lobby who had just walked in and was impatient to speak to her cousin. He then walked over and introduced himself to Sarah as Dolphus Hinkel and said, "May I have a word with your friend?"

"My friend is my cousin," Sarah said.

"How charming," said Dolphus Hinkel.

"Yes, how charming," Sarah said.

Egon said to her, "Would you mind excusing us for a just a moment?"

"Only for a moment," Sarah allowed.

They stepped aside. Dolphus Hinkel said to Egon, "He's not here."

"Who's not here?"

"von Feffenhausen."

"Didn't you meet him at the station?"

"He wasn't there," Dolphus Hinkel said. "And I've checked every inn in town."

"He must be somewhere."

"You didn't see him on the train?"

"I was on the last train out of Berlin," Egon said, "and he was to have been on the one before that."

"Maybe von Feffenhausen changed his mind."

"No," Egon said. "This is about self-interest. If you can understand that in a man, then you can trust him up until that self-interest changes, and it was in von Feffenhausen's interest to align with us. Now, what exactly happened in Hamburg?"

Dolphus Hinkel said, "Everyone aboard ship was killed—you don't think that von Feffenhausen was arrested?"

"What matters is that von Coors will never get near the munitions."

Dolphus Hinkel said, "But what if von Feffenhausen should make a deal with the police and talk?"

"Does he have the keys?"

"I've got people working on making new ones at this very moment."

Egon said, "Well, for all we know he got hit by a car."

"Maybe that's what von Feffenhausen wants us to think."

"What are you suggesting?"

Dolphus Hinkel said, "It's not what I'm suggesting, but what I'm concluding."

"And what is that?"

"We could be walking straight into a trap tonight," Dolphus Hinkel said.

"I think you're overreacting."

"What if von Feffenhausen is still with von Coors, or has been arrested and is making some kind of deal with the government?"

"Just because von Feffenhausen wasn't elected Party Chairman?"

Dolphus Hinkel said, "He's been unhappy. Everyone knows that. Von Coors may have started the party, but Hitler was invited into his and then took it over, and that's what von Feffenhausen is thinking."

Egon said, "Without a line of cash, nothing will be his."

"We know that, but does he? I mean, some men are truly delusional."

Before Egon could answer that, Beau entered the lobby with his saxophone case in hand. Egon was surprised to see how friendly he was with Sarah.

Dolphus Hinkel said to Egon, "Seems your cousin has a nigger boyfriend."

Sarah, fully aware of the unwelcome stares, quietly said to Beau, "The tall man over there is my cousin Egon von Remmele. He speaks English as well as I, so I need you to pretend that you're my servant."

Beau said, "That's what a servant does best."

Egon came over and said to Sarah in German, "I thought you were travelling alone."

"Alone means without family, but I am with friends."

"This monkey is your friend?"

"Egon, when a woman says that she's traveling alone, it doesn't mean without her servants."

"You just said friends."

"And I also said servants. You of all people should know that. Now, let's sit down somewhere. The lobby is no place to talk."

Egon said, "I'm sorry, but I have an appointment right at this moment."

Sarah didn't believe him but said, "Then we'll meet for supper, in half an hour, because I have something to tell you that you'll find *very* interesting; this is not the place."

"Well, I'm not sure that I can make supper, either," Egon said.

"Are you turning me down?"

"No, of course not, Sarah, but you can surely understand the pressing matters of a man's business."

"Nonsense, I have the most charming place for supper."

"I'm pressed for time, Sarah."

"One doesn't go without supper. Now, let's dine in that charming restaurant in the castle."

"The castle…?"

"Yes."

"Down the street?"

"Yes," Sarah said.

Egon knew that there wasn't a restaurant in the castle and said, "I suppose you've made reservations."

"I'll make them now," Sarah said, "and for a table with a splendid view. You'll be able to see your bankers all the way over in Switzerland and wave to them."

Henni walked into the lobby and said to Beau in German, "Here's your costume. Meet us at the town hall by the Count Johann von Hohenzollern-Sigmaringen market fountain when the music starts and don't forget to bring your saxophone."

Egon leaned into Sarah and said, "Servants now play the saxophone?"

"Oh, he's good at a lot of things…"

56

The Boilers

Heinz and Fritz brought the Keeper of Keys into one of the castle's windowless rooms. They put on brass knuckles that ringed each finger and then clenched their fists to make them fit.

Heinz approached the Keeper of Keys. "Where are the girls?"

"I do not know," the Keeper of Keys said, still wanting to be brave.

Heinz crushed his nose and then his jaw. The Keeper of Keys fell to the floor. "Where are the girls…?" but the Keeper of Keys wouldn't talk. They beat him again. Still, he wouldn't talk. Heinz removed a sharp heavy bladed hunting knife from its sheaf and stabbed it into the top of the keeper's hand, not once, but twice, and then drew it down into his fingers and cut them off.

The Keeper of Keys had had enough of being brave.

"Did you find him?" Otto Zumbach said to Heinz and Fritz as they entered the crown prince chamber.

"Yeah."

"The girls?"

"He hid them."

"Where?"

"The boiler room."

"Are they back in the tower?"

"Yeah."

"Good," Otto Zumbach said. "Get rid of him and the Jewess. The other one stays in the tower—and *do not* touch her."

Heinz and Fritz left the chamber.

The telephone rang.

Otto Zumbach took it and recognized the voice on the other end of the line. "When did you get here?"

"Just now," Egon said. "I've been trying to reach you."

"I had to step out-—and Hinkel?"

"He met me at the inn," Egon said.

"We have a problem."

"What?"

Otto Zumbach said, "Von Feffenhausen was on his way from Berlin, but he never got off the train."

"How do you know that he was on the train?"

"Because my men spoke to the train conductor who told them that von Feffenhausen had been onboard."

"Are you sure about that?"

"The conductor described him to a T."

Egon said, "The conductor could've been paid off by him to say that."

"He could have," Otto Zumbach said.

"When did you speak to von Feffenhausen last?"

Otto Zumbach said, "He called me before he left Berlin and told me that he was on his way and that he had spoken to you."

"He left a note," Egon said. "He did not speak to me."

"What did you two talk about?"

"I just told you," Egon said. "He left me a note. We did not talk. There was nothing to talk about."

"What did it say?" Otto said.

"Are you sure that he's not in the castle?"

"Herr Remmele, von Feffenhausen is nowhere to be found. What did he say to you when you spoke to him?"

"I'll be up at the castle at the appointed hour," Egon said, "and we'll talk about it then, not here in some lobby……"

57

The Pit

Heinz unlocked the tower door and headed straight to Ilse. "So, you're the famous Voodoo Child."

Fritz told Heinz, "Not now."

Heinz, annoyed, said, "I haven't done a thing."

"You were about to," Fritz said, as took hold of Ilse.

Shelby slipped her pocketbook into Ilse's coat and said to her, in English, "It's loaded......"

The Ford-Werke sedan crossed the Danube River and continued on until it reached an old country lane that led to the Schwarzwald. Heinz said to Fritz, who was in the back seat with Ilse, "This all looks the same to me. You sure you know where we are?"

"I'm sure," said Fritz.

"Nothing but trees."

"Stop the car."

"Now?"

"*Stop* it," said Fritz.

The sedan halted by the edge of the forest. Fritz opened the door and pulled Ilse out of the back seat. Her hands were tied behind her. Heinz took the Keeper of Keys, who was wrapped inside a sheet, and put him over his shoulder. Heinz said, "You sure you know where we are in this darkness?"

Fritz ignored him and struck a match over a military compass and said, "We're on course at 160 degrees." They headed into the Black Forest, thick with trees and mossy rocks that were easy to slip over. Fritz attached a bicycle lantern to his coat and, as it swung back and forth, the trees seemed to sway weirdly with it. He kept one arm inside Ilse's so that she couldn't get away. They went on like this for another 20 minutes before Fritz stopped. He aimed the lantern at some clear ground and then attached it to a high branch to light up the area. He handed Ilse to Heinz and then kneeled down and cleared away the dirt. He pulled back a few old planks that covered a pit. Deep inside, despite the cold air, was a swarming cloud of gnats and black blowflies feasting on Zola's rotting corpse. Heinz tossed the Keeper of Keys into the pit alongside her. Ilse, seizing the moment, tried to run off into the forest, but Heinz grabbed her and threw her to the ground. He wasted little time as he pulled back her dress and then her underwear. She said to him, "It would be easier if you untied me."

Heinz stared at her for a moment. "Why would you want to make it easier?"

"Because I'll break my wrists, if you can understand that."

Heinz cut the rope and then pushed her back onto the ground. When he was done, he got up and said to Fritz, "Your turn," but then a strange look came over Heinz's face, that of someone who had lived a second too long. Gunfire woke the forest and turned it into a rattling pitch of coos and cries. Ilse then put the gun on Fritz who said, "You won't be able to get out of the forest on your own. Come with me. I *will not* hurt you. I'm not like Heinz."

"Then why didn't you stop him from raping me?"

"He would have killed me."

"And so you allowed him to rape me."

"…I'm sorry."

It sounded good, but gunfire sounded even better. She blew out his brains and took the compass, their guns, the key to the sedan, the lantern, and pushed the dead men into the pit and covered it. She then headed west, at roughly 320 degrees, and navigated the maze of dense trees that proved as disagreeable as the ground was uneven. Every so often she had to stop and take a new reading as each rocky step acted to drift her off-course. Within the hour, and what seemed forever, Ilse finally found the black Ford-Werke sedan flinching under the glow of the lantern's light. She got into the car and drove back to Sigmaringen, at one moment crying and the next furious for the filth that was now inside her.

58

The Origin of the World

"How do you know the costume won't fit?" Sarah said to Beau as they entered her room in the Deutsches Haus Inn. "Try it on and see."

Beau reached into the bag that Henni had brought him and took out the giant top hat with the scary hands attached to the sides that extended a meter and flapped back and forth. "Go ahead. It won't bite you," Sarah said, sitting down and tossing her legs over the side of the big chair.

"I'll look like an idiot," he said.

Sarah kicked off her shoes and said, "You haven't put it on yet, so how do you know?"

He put on the big crazy hat and looked in the mirror and said, "I couldn't believe you told your cousin that there was a restaurant in the castle."

"The fool didn't even know there wasn't one, unless I'm wrong," Sarah said. "Reminds me of my late husband."

"How's that?" Beau said, taking another part of the costume that he wasn't sure how to put on.

Sarah said, "I'd tell him I'm meeting friends for a milk shake at the top of the Statue of Liberty and the fool would say okay."

"Maybe he wasn't listenin'."

"He never listened to me from the day we got married."

"Then why did you marry him?"

"Since when is marriage about liking someone?"

"Well, most folks think it is," Beau said, putting on a strange orange buttoned purple jacket that flared out over his legs.

Sarah laughed and said, "You look like a scarecrow."

"I feel like one," Beau said, as he took off the jacket and slipped on a bright yellow vest with mint green pompoms. "Why did you marry him then?"

"His family passed the social test."

"What test was that?"

Sarah said, "They had social standing, but no money, unlike his cousins here in Germany, and so his people wanted him to marry into my family to get back up to speed. Unfortunately, I impressed them, and they impressed my family, but not for long, and by then it was too late." She then sat up and squared her hands and looked through them. "I wish I'd brought my paint box. I'm really in the mood to paint."

"Maybe they sell 'em in town," Beau said as he fidgeted with the gold buckled shoes.

"Good luck with that," Sarah said, using her hands to frame what she saw in her mind's eye. "Do you paint…?"

"No, ma'am, I don't." Beau took out the rest of the costume, not sure if the pants were pants or a shirt with very long sleeves.

Sarah said, "Well, after hearing you play that horn of yours, there's no doubt you're a talented fella. Maybe you should give it a try and see what happens."

"Well, music is one thing, but I don't think the two's related."

Sarah moved her left arm through the air, as if a paint brush were in her hand. "I'd like to paint me."

"You, ma'am…?"

"Yeah, me," she said.

"Kinda hard paintin' yourself."

Sarah got up off the couch and said, "Where's that camera of yours?"

"In my coat pocket. Why?"

"Get it."

"What for?"

"I've got a brilliant idea," she said, as she undid her dress.

"You got another spot to clean?"

"No," Sarah said, standing in her teddy, her bare arms and legs getting in the way of Beau's vision.

"What about that Feffenhausen fella?"

"What about him?"

"You mentioned that your cousin was talkin' about him downstairs in the lobby."

"Which only proves what was done to him was the right thing to do," Sarah said.

"You sure about that?" Beau said, taking the Leica 1A out of his coat pocket."

"Absolutely. We're dealing with tyrants, people who believe there is only one way to live and that it's their way, which requires complete submission inevitably entailing violence against those whom they consider to be in opposition or unworthy."

"You mean you're justifyin' what was done to Wolfie."

"What was done to him, Beau, was not based on some perverted ideology nor grab for power, but what a surgeon does when a part of the body is no longer functioning; if it's beyond repair, then it must be excised, and that is what was done to von Feffenhausen."

"Well, ma'am, he might say the same thing to you."

"And he would say that you're a dumb nigger."

"…You got a point there," Beau admitted, as he showed her the camera.

"Now, since I can't take pictures of myself, you're going to take them of me."

"I am…?"

"Yes," Sarah said. "See, I'm going to do a proper painting like the old masters did, so that I'll be considered a real genius of an artist and the fools won't ignore me anymore. I doubt you'd know about that painting by Gustave Corbet."

"Which painting, ma'am?"

"Well, I haven't really seen it myself," Sarah said, "but my grandmother had a friend who had gotten a real close look at it before it went missing for years. Then when I was old enough and ready, she told me all about it."

"*Old* enough and ready, ma'am…?"

"Yes," Sarah said, looking away.

"Old enough for what, ma'am?"

"Well, you see the subject of Corbet's painting just happens to be of a woman lying on a bed in a certain position."

"What kinda position?"

Sarah said, "One that makes your eyes get big."

"How big…?"

"Let's just say that the title of the painting is "The Origin of the World," and it's the most honest nude ever done, as far as I'm concerned."

"I'm guessin' it's more than jus' nude."

"Oh, yes," Sarah said, using her hands to frame the midsection of her body. "It confronts a certain part of the naked body and then gives you the choice of seeing it as pornographic or as something mysteriously tied to creation, and the choice that you make reveals who you are. The French understand this. They can look at the bare human body without acting like a toad, but for us Americans we wet our pants," Sarah said, slipping off her teddy, then her stockings and garters, leaving them helter-skelter on the floor. She hopped on the bed and spread her legs, just as in Courbet's painting. "…What're you waiting for?

"Well, uh, ma'am, just how do you want these pictures taken?"

"Like I showed you."

"I, uh…I don't remember."

Sarah said, "From below my breasts to the tip of my thighs and make sure that my vagina is centered in the frame as in Courbet's painting. Just my body, not my head."

"…You sure of that?"

"Yeah, I'm sure," Sarah said, and then without nuance, "Unless you've got something better in mind……"

59

Don't Be Afraid

Ilse crossed over the Danube River bridge into Sigmaringen, drove through the narrow backstreets and parked the sedan where it could not be found easily. She then searched the ancient winding streets, now under light snowfall, for the Deutsches Haus where Mr. Benchley had said that everyone was staying. She found it soon enough and asked the concierge, in German, if Mr. Benchley was in. The concierge told her that he hadn't yet returned. Ilse then told him that she was staying with her Aunt Sarah and wanted the key to the room. The concierge did not doubt that Ilse was telling the truth. He gave her the key to the room. Ilse hurried upstairs and, after knocking several times, opened the door with the key. Once inside, she found Sarah's trunk emptied, her clothes scattered all over the floor, but no sign of her. Ilse headed back to the lobby and asked the concierge if he knew where Mrs. Remley had gone for the evening. "To the Fastnacht parade, where else?" he said, moving on to the next guest who was dressed up in a costume of a gigantic pig's head with an enormous cigar in its mouth and a drooping tongue. Ilse left the inn and followed a crowd of people on their way to the base of the Count Johann von Hohenzollern-Sigmaringen market fountain in the town square. She inquired if they had seen or heard any Americans, but no one had. She then felt a tap on her shoulder. A woman, with unkempt long gray hair and a voice as distant as her eyes, said, "We've been waiting for you."

Ilse said to her, "We met on the other side."

"We did," Elke said, as she gave Ilse a costume with a stained wooden mask and crooked lips. "

"How did you know that I'd be here?"

Elke said, "Our father's house has many mansions, but then you're a Norn and you already know that."

"You mean dimensions."

"As you like," Elke said.

"I'm not a Norn."

"Then what are you?"

"How did you know that I'd be crossing over the other day?"

Elke said, "Knowledge on the other side is not temporal, as you already know. Now, the carnival has started. So, hurry up and get your costume on."

Ilse put on the long red high heeled boots and the blood red cape with its black hood that was attached to the wooden mask. "And why is this red?"

"You're the Voodoo Child."

"I thought I was a Norn," Ilse said.

"They're one in the same. Now, hurry. The parade will lead you to where you are going as everything else has done in your life."

Ilse adjusted her cape. "You're sure about that?"

Elke said to her, "You forget what you know and when you know it, you forget that you forgot it—you'll get used to it."

"You mean like being on that ocean liner that I took across the Atlantic."

"Yes, in that once you're onboard, all you can really do is choose what's on the menu." Elke pointed the way. "There's no time to waste. Hurry. You know where to go."

"But there is nowhere to go. The die has already been cast. You know that as well as I."

Elke said, "There's still that menu……."

60

A Lesson

The Austrian's Mercedes 11/40 pulled to a stop inside the castle's bailey. Hitler stepped out and was greeted by Egon who took him to the DNF's chamber, "…and what about the ship in Hamburg?"

Egon lied to him, "The French are behind what happened in Hamburg. It's their ship, and their ability to use deceit to make us suffer has no ends. You haven't forgotten how they kicked and beat our people in the Ruhr back in '23 if we didn't salute or take off our hats when we walked past them. All the workers in my factories haven't forgotten that and I know that neither have you. Whoever killed that French officer, no man of honor and dignity would have blamed a whole people. But then that's what we're up against: liars and Jews."

"Where's von Feffenhausen?"

Egon said, "He was delayed."

"What happened?"

Egon said, "Oh, it's most probably that recurring infection from his old war wound. It's been a real problem lately."

"What about von Coors?"

"He's leading the Fastnacht parade—is your man ready?"

"Ready and waiting," Hitler said, "but I need to know that von Feffenhausen is with us and not behind what happened in Hamburg, because that would mean he lied to us and is still with the DNF."

"I already told you what happened," Egon said.

"I know you have, Herr von Remmele. I'm just reminding you as we often forget things."

"He's with us," Egon said.

"Have you spoken to Hugenberg?"

"Yes," Egon said, "and he's using his network of newspapers to clear up that little problem with the Ellis Remley letter."

"Well, he'd better do a good job of it," Hitler said, "because the government and everyone else has concluded from the letter that you were behind the shipment as well."

"And that's why I want you to have a word with Hugenberg," Egon said.

"You mean about the two girls?"

"Not only that, but to hear it from himself how the Soviets forged the letter. He'll be publishing what Stalin did to clear our names."

"Stalin forged the letter…?"

"Absolutely," Egon lied.

"I like that, and I have something else to speak to Hugenberg about."

"And what is that?"

"You'll hear it when he gets on the phone," Hitler said.

"Is it about the letter?"

"That and something else," Hitler said.

Egon said, "Well, at this very moment, the Stalin letter is being typeset for the front pages of the morning editions of every newspaper that Hugenberg owns and it will prove that the Remley letter was a fake, but the real charm of it is that all the Berlin papers will have to print the letter because it will be the new leading story in Germany, and this will further inoculate us."

"And what's in the letter?"

Egon said, "That it was written to the leader of the Reds here and signed by Stalin, ordering his agents to sabotage German industry, first through propaganda, then by insurrection. The letter includes the directive for the making of the forgery of the Ellis Remley letter to Hugenberg."

"But we already know that the Reds, through Stalin, are trying to take over our country."

Egon stopped him and said, "That's the whole point. Common knowledge is what matters, not the truth. Now come along, we're almost there……"

61

Soundproof

"**. . . I** look ridiculous."

"You look terrific," Ziggy said to her brother, as she adjusted the gigantic black head with its little pink hat attached on top. Peepholes were hidden inside the two big yellow eyes for the Major to see through. He wore orange mittens with glittering fingertips, knickerbocker pants with long royal blue socks, and giant black shoes with shiny silver bells that jingled as he walked. "In fact, you've never looked better in your life."

"Otto was supposed to have called me from the castle."

"You'll see him later," Ziggy said.

"He was supposed to have called."

"You just spoke to him."

"I have to speak to him again."

"Forget about him," Ziggy said.

The phone rang.

"That's Frau Kleister," Ziggy said.

"Maybe it's Otto."

Ziggy picked up the telephone in the hall and then said to the Major, "It's Frau Kleister."

The Major shouted, "Tell her to go to hell."

Ziggy spoke to her for a moment and then returned to the bedroom. "I told her that we're on the way. Now, let's go. I've got papa's touring car up and running."

"How the hell am I going to fit inside an automobile?"

Ziggy said, "We'll find a way. The leader of the carnival always arrives in costume." She guided her brother out of the bedroom, down the wall, and somehow through the front door. She then stuffed him into their father's Steiger 11/55 touring car and drove down the long dirt path that led to town.

The Major yelled, under the nearly soundproof costume, "*Stop!*"

"We're late, Magnus. We don't have time to play around."

"*Stop* the goddamn car!" the Major said, reaching for the ignition.

Ziggy tried to push his hand away. "The hell are you doing?"

He cut the motor, opened the passenger door, and squeezed himself out of the car and tipped over onto the ground. Ziggy had to get him up. "Magnus, you're acting like a child."

"I'm taking off this goddamn costume."

"*No*, you're not, Magnus."

"Yes, I am, and *you're* going to wear it."

"I'm not the leader of the parade this year. *You* are." Ziggy said.

"No one will know the difference."

"Frau Kleister will."

"Fuck her…"

62

The Crown Prince Chamber

Otto Zumbach tried to be agreeable as he stood before the flag of the Deutsche Nationale Freiheitspartei that covered the chamber wall. He said to the Austrian, "The Major emphatically told me that nothing's to be done until he gets here. You understand that I have to respect his wishes."

The Austrian said, "*Get* Hugenberg on the phone. I'll deal with the Major."

Egon gently put his hand on Hitler's arm and then said to Otto Zumbach, "I'm the one paying for everything here. So, all you have to do is pick up the telephone and get Hugenberg on the line, unless you want to start footing the bill yourselves."

Otto Zumbach unhooked the candlestick telephone and waited for the operator to put a connection through to Berlin. When the line came through, he handed the receiver to Egon who said, "Emil…? Yes, good evening… Yes, I've heard… Let them say whatever they want. That will all soon change… I understand… That's why I'm here… Of course, she's alive… And you can tell Nachman that he'll have her back shortly… That's why I'm here… Good… No, he's here right beside me… Yes, I will… Just a moment, now."

Egon handed the telephone to Hitler, who said, "Good evening, Herr Hugenberg… Yes, this is he… No, not at all… Yes, we just arrived… I understand.… Well, before you print that letter from Stalin,

I want you to first run the story of the kidnapped American girl… Let me explain… No, we just need to shift the focus of the news from the Ellis Remley letter for a day, maybe two… Of course, I understand your situation, but before Stalin's letter is printed… If you'd *listen*, sir… I want my rescue of the American girl and photographs of me and her to be the lead story… Absolutely, and I'll have the film flown right up in a Fokker F.VII, but the photographs must be published on the front page… No, no, I'm not at all saying ditch the Stalin letter story, but first we must condition the public about the compassion and decency of the leader of the NSDAP and only then do we run the story about Stalin's malicious letter alongside it… Of course, von Remmele knows about it… Well, if Frau Remley is stupid enough to refute the Stalin letter, we have photos of her totally naked with her gorgeous legs up in the air getting fucked by a nigger, and when people see that she'll lose all credibility… No, the negatives haven't been developed, yet… Is she cute?... Ohh, you mean can she *get* cute… Well, I haven't met her yet… I can assure you that she was naked… Well, they certainly weren't playing Parcheesi… Well, if that's the case then we'll have to publish the photos of her before she has a chance to refute the Stalin letter… Well, *only* if she opens her mouth then, if not I want the photos of her and the American girl getting rescued by me to be published tomorrow and then the pictures of her fucking her cute little ass off *if* she refutes our claims." The former corporal gestured to Egon that he was about to finish up the call. "Herr Hugenberg, you needn't say another word about the Major… I know that he treated you like shit, but we Nazis aren't like that. We do things differently…"

63

The Spell

The Major dropped Ziggy off at Frau Kleister's timber house in town, and then drove up to the castle. Elke, dressed in her black witch's Fastnacht hat, was coming down the hill. She said to him, "The Norns have arrived."

The Major got out of the car and said, "How did you get up here so fast?"

"Never mind how I got here, Magnus. The Voodoo Child was a gift from the Deities, and you tried to kill her."

"Frau Kleister, you gave me a Jewess."

"Do not call me that here."

"I'll call you what I want," said the Major.

Elke said, "She could have been the voice and wisdom of your movement had you not been such a childish fool."

"Frau Kleister, a woman, let alone a teenager, does not lead a movement."

"Then I have nothing more say to you."

"*Wait*. Don't go, yet. Do you have your bag of spells with you?"

"I've used them once already, for you, and look what you've done."

"Well, you're going to use them again, old witch, and cast another spell, but one stronger and everlasting, because I have lost my patience with you. Now come along," the Major said, shoving her into his car.

"Where are you taking me?"

"To the forest where the magic is done. Where else…?"

The Major drove across the Danube River bridge and continued on for several kilometers until they reached the very edge of the Black Forest. He got out of the touring car and took Elke into the dense mass of trees with a lantern in one hand and his army compass in the other. He had little patience as he trekked over the mossy slippery rocks that were cobbled in-between trees and shrubs which did little to deflect the ornery hungry sounds that came at them from every side of the deep and dark Schwarzwald. They stumbled, slipped, and were snagged and pinched by thorns and branches on ground that treacherously dipped and dropped. Further on, he stopped and circled the lantern over the ground and kicked away the dirt. He removed the cover of the pit. In the wavering light, he saw Heinz and Fritz, the Keeper of Keys, and Zola's bloated body infested with feasting vermin anxious to get to their next meal.

"You're a murderer," Elke said.

The Major ignored her.

"I've known you since you were a boy. Always full of pride. Always dreaming."

"You have yet to see what I'll do… Now, where's the Jewess?"

"Magnus, a Norn does as she likes, but in years to come this pit shall be one of many thousands filled with dead, until there's a place to bury the lies that you people spread." Elke reached into her leather pouch that hung off the rope of her coarse witch's dress and said, "You asked for a spell and so I will cast you one and we shall see what it portends." She spread the elements from her pouch across the pit and said, "This spell has never been cast nor been put into words until this very moment." She stood at the edge of the pit, opened her hands and cast the spell:

> "Powdered nails of blinded beggars,
> Prince's eyelash, one thief 's tongue,

Salted lies and pauper's porridge,
Two parts dog hair flees 'n fangs,
All inside a candle lit skull,
Worn for a month, unbathed and left to dull,
To be drunk from the widow's spoon,
Then scattered into the mist of foulest breath,
Boiled in slips of sage,
Simmered in hogs' hair and boiled again,
Singing aye, aye, eye for an eye,
Until the stillborn cry and you have long died."

A large cloud of smoke snapped up from the bottom of the pit and when it cleared it was empty of anything before. Then trembling voices howled from every direction of the forest and shook everything underfoot. When this passed, Elke and the Major rose up from the ground. She took the lantern and said, "The tide of time has risen."

"What about me being ruler of Germany?"

"That's where the carnage lies," Elke said.

"You were to cast a spell to make me ruler and nothing else."

"Magnus, a real spell is not to fulfil some wish of we want to happen, but a disclosure of what we refuse to see, good or bad."

"Not as far as I'm concerned."

"Then understand this: The future is not in your reach anymore, but in someone else's; someone worse than you."

"Frau Kleister, I can cast spells, too."

The Major then drew his gun and shot her dead.

64

You Know This Clown?

Beau, Sarah, and Shelby were brought down from the tower and introduced to the former corporal. Egon did the honors. "This is my cousin Sarah Revenlöw Remley and this is Fräulein Prevette. Ladies, meet Herr Hitler." Beau was ignored.

The Austrian took Shelby's hand and made a courtly bow. "A pleasure to meet you, Fräulein." He did the same with Sarah and said, "Your cousin was modest in his description of you."

"He has good manners or bad eyesight," Sarah said.

The Austrian marveled at Sarah's high cheekbones and gentle blue eyes and so he missed the determination behind them. "You both speak German quite well."

"We try," Shelby said.

Egon reminded her, "Herr Hitler is the one who freed you two from captivity."

Sarah said to the Austrian, "And what motivated you?"

"Two noble women in danger. Need I say more? Are you both of German blood?"

"You aren't," said Sarah.

Hitler taken aback, said, "I'm 100% German."

"Your accent isn't," Sarah said.

"I was born in Austria, but we're all Germans."

"You're sure of that?"

"As sure as a silver fir tree in Bavaria is the same as any other in Austria or Switzerland."

"Yes," Sarah said, "but you're not a tree—or are you?"

"No," the former corporal said, trying to hold his smile. "But, then, a beautiful woman may be excused of what she says." He stared at Egon wanting to know why he hadn't been warned about her sharp tongue.

Sarah said to Egon, in English, "You know this clown?"

"Yes, so please hold your wit."

"I would never let go of it," she said.

Hitler said to Sarah, "I heard a ghastly rumor that you may wish to dispel."

"Rumors are for those who gossip."

Hitler said, "Gossip which concerns social issues is no longer gossip."

"Well, without it, it couldn't be gossip."

"Gossip or not," Hitler said, "is this nigger really your boyfriend?"

"It's the truth, not a rumor."

"I love it when a woman lies to make a point," Hitler said.

"We weren't having sex, if that's what's worrying you."

"Then what were you having?"

Sarah said, "I can't photograph myself."

"…I don't understand."

"It's a long story," Sarah said.

"I'm listening."

"I needed someone to take my photo."

"Then why not get a woman who could protect your decency?"

"My decency was not at risk," Sarah said.

"It is, if it's in question."

"Then your motivation should be in question," Sarah said, and then to Egon in English, "What's his problem?"

"He sees the world in a certain way."

"I *know* that, and you support it?"

"Concerning industry, yes," Egon said, "but then no one is perfect."

"And some are way less than perfect," Sarah said, turning back to the Austrian. "I'll explain, so that you'll understand. I'm a painter working on a project about a naked woman lying on a bed—you do know of Gustave Courbet's work of art?"

"Whether I do or not," Hitler said, "you should have had a woman taking your photograph."

"Beau was already there," Sarah said.

"You send him off."

"There was no one else," Sarah said.

"You could've asked the concierge to have found you a woman."

"You're missing the point," Sarah said.

"What point?"

"My concern is that you look at yourself differently than you would at someone else. All those little flaws. Those little nasty things that escape you, but no one else—*if* you know what I mean."

Hitler said, "Well, as an artist, I know that painting yourself also has the burden of potential dishonesty in that you'll leave out all the things that you don't like, contrary to what you say."

Sarah said, "If you're a lousy artist, yes, but not if you're a real one. Think of Van Gogh's self-portraits, or Rembrandt's, the shock of seeing themselves for the first time is apparent in each stroke. Rather than avoiding the truth they embraced it without exaggeration, as I assume you or any great artist would."

"Yes, but they were of long ago. The art of today, I wouldn't even call art," Hitler said.

"I'm not talking about today's art."

"I am, Frau Remley, and the incomprehensible art of today is nothing but self-indulgent degenerate nonsense. The French notion that a lack of talent *is* talent has allowed cranks and the Jew to warrant ugliness and ineptitude into art and culture, which is why Picasso and his ilk play with your mind by saying that *you* can't see what they can, when there's nothing there to see."

"And just what makes your opinion more informed than anyone else's?"

"I just told you, Frau Remley."

"You complained is all that you did, and that comes from a murkier source."

"Then understand this," Hitler said, "I would never be foolish enough to consider degeneracy as art, as it not only lacks personal courage, but it undermines our people."

"Then you need to understand that personal courage is also admitting your weaknesses, which we all suffer."

"But that's not art," Hitler said, closing his fist.

"It becomes art."

"It's *lying* art."

Sarah said, "The art of lying is another kind of art, which you well understand."

"No, I don't, but what I do understand is that Society women are to be prized for their wit, despite their ignorance."

"Really…? Do you come from Society? Because I don't ever remember hearing your name."

"I *don't* come from Society," Hitler said, "but attractive women know that they can say the wildest of things and be fêted for it, when a man would be shot."

"Then you'd have been shot long ago," Sarah said.

"I'm talking about something else."

"You always are…Oh, and by the way, there are people who fought as valiantly as you in the war, who would disagree with all of your notions, including about art."

"You cannot be valiant and disagree with what I say," said Hitler. "It would be a contradiction."

"Your insistence is based neither on logic nor fact, therefore you're open to attack, so get used to it," Sarah said.

"Then you should read my book and learn something, before you go on the attack."

"I couldn't get through it," Sarah said.

"Are you a slow reader?"

"Not at all," Sarah said. "Actually, I'm very fast, but I had to read it to my husband and translate it at the same time, and I found it curious, if not surprising, that you well understood that propaganda has nothing to do with the truth. What matters is how you manipulate someone with lies for *your* benefit, while claiming that it's for his, but then talking to you is like the rest of your book, you have a vision, but one that exists way outside of reality."

"You think you're clever," Hitler said, "but wit is too often an excuse for insight, which you obviously lack."

"Is that because you think I'm stupid?"

"You come from money, Frau Remley. You've never struggled."

"A man who's used to docile women has never engaged in battle."

"You know nothing of battle."

"I know the limitations of war; men don't."

"You don't understand men."

"Whoever has…?"

Hitler said, in retreat, "I would've liked to have met the man who married you."

"So would have I," Sarah said.

"…I don't understand."

"I wouldn't let that worry you."

"Are you still in mourning?"

"In more ways than one," Sarah said.

"And how is that?"

Sarah said, "I mourn less for someone having died than the waste of his ever having lived."

"On the contrary, your husband was a man who loved the Fatherland."

"He also dreamed while standing on one foot."

"That could be a good thing, as well," said the Austrian.

"If you only have one leg."

"Well, had your husband been here, I have no doubt that you'd be behaving differently."

"Really…..? I suppose that you're in the employment of Dr. Freud?"

"That Jew is an idiot."

"He would say the same of you," Sarah said.

"He can say what he wants, but what matters is who has the final word."

"And I can assure you that I will have it."

"Frau Remley, with a face like yours, a man has to accept whatever you say, and there lies the accommodation of love and what it spoils."

"Then you must never have loved."

Hitler said, "Enough of this," and snapped his fingers. A tray of tea and chocolate creampuffs were rolled in. Egon put down the candlestick telephone and came over to whisper in the former corporal's ear. "They've just left…"

65

Magic Dust

The Austrian's Mercedes 11/40 drove through the castle portcullis and down the steep narrow hill. Minutes later it turned into a side street, away from the parade, and parked. The man in the passenger seat got out of the car. He pulled out a black reversible cape, a wooden mask with an accentuated nose and chin, and a large black three-cornered hat. He reached under the seat for a flat case. He took it out and removed the gun suppressor, attached it to the end of his pistol, and slipped it inside his cape. The driver said, "I'll be waiting here." The man with the suppressor disappeared into the dark narrow streets. Under the flurry of snow, he found the parade and blended in.

66

Cuckoo

Mr. Benchley closed his Baedeker guidebook, 19th ed. *Paris and its Environs,* 1924, and left the Deutsches Haus Sitting Room for the front desk. He asked the concierge if Mrs. Remley had returned. The concierge said, "Not yet, sir, otherwise I would have called you."

"She didn't leave me a note?"

"I would have given it to you."

Mr. Benchley, not knowing what to do, returned to the sitting room with its quaint paintings of country life. A woman dressed as a flying hen entered with great difficulty and gave stern words to her husband who was inside a huge goose egg with his head sticking out the middle. The cuckoo bird popped out of the wall clock and went cuckoo. Mr. Benchley had had enough of waiting.

67

Fastnacht

Brass horns voiced the midnight hour. Paraders reached out into the crowd with hollowed hammers, staves, and bells. The man in the black cape and three-cornered hat paid no mind.

68

Creampuff

The Major, having just returned from the Black Forest, stopped his father's Steiger 11/55 touring car just short of the castle's portcullis. He was told that he would have to wait before entering.

The Major said, "I've never seen you here before."

"I was instructed that no one enters tonight without clearance. Your name, sir?"

"Santa Claus," the Major said.

"I need your real name."

"That is my real name," the Major said, pressing a Pistole-Parabellum to the man's head. The portcullis was opened.

It was now a race to see who would get to the chocolate creampuffs first. Sarah grabbed a plump one that Hitler had his eye on and gave it to Beau. She said to the former corporal, "Don't you tire of all this blood and purity stuff?"

"Do housewives tire of brooms and disinfectants?"

"Well, you'll need more than a broom to do what you're planning," Sarah said. "And your taking four baths a day is highly obsessive and is obviously tied to this need of yours to clean up the world of its so-called vermin, which is nothing but your fear of germs, but then the Right has always had this obsession with cleaning house, much more than housewives."

"Nonsense. And just what am I planning?"

"Read your book," Sarah said.

The former corporal sucked the powdered sugar off of each finger and said, "I see your nigger likes creampuffs."

"So do you," Sarah said, grabbing another creampuff and giving it to Beau.

"The problem is that a woman reads differently from a man," Hitler said, his eyes on Beau.

"Cite me evidence of that."

"You're the evidence, unless of course you understood my book."

"I couldn't stand it," Sarah said. "Especially all that baloney about a leader having absolute power."

Hitler said, "You of all people would love absolute power, if you had it."

"What're you implying?"

"I'm implying that you need a single leader to make decisions in government as the parliamentary system is nothing but a mess. They squabble like a bunch of sissies and get nothing done. It's all in my book."

"Your book is what's a mess," Sarah said.

"Then you haven't read it."

"Oh, but I have."

"Then the translation wasn't any good."

"I read it in German, as I have already told you," Sarah said, "and you came across as insufferably intolerant."

"Intolerant of stupidity."

"But not of intolerance."

"I *saved* your life."

"And in doing so, you saved my opinions, including my utter distaste for your notion of killing people based on childish notions of blood."

"It's cleansing," Hitler said, "which is a little different."

"Cleansing…? I thought only housewives do that," Sarah said, handing Beau another creampuff. "Though I did find your chapter on propaganda interesting, if unoriginal—my late husband was in advertising and quite often spoke as you have written."

"And just what did you like about it?"

"That propaganda must be attuned to the limited intelligence of the masses, which demands that a message be simplified and emotionally rooted and not put forth to please the scholars. The key is in understanding that a mass's receptivity is severely limited if you try to talk or debate with each person in it. You need to reach the masses by exploiting shared emotions, not debate whether an issue is right or wrong, because you'll only weaken your message. In other words, propaganda is *not* the objective study of what is true, otherwise we'd call it truth. Propaganda is messaging as debating is deconstructing the message, and that difference is what's lost on the smart folks. On the other hand, you, and I, here, are pressured to debate all sides of an issue, because sloganeering in small groups comes off as condescending, but, then, it hasn't stopped you from doing that."

The former corporal looked at the empty creampuff tray and said to Shelby, "You took the last one."

Shelby said, "Who's counting?"

Sarah said, "He is," and then to Hitler, "And your notions about the world are nothing new as human nature, evidenced by history, may change its mustache, but not its vile ambitions. I'll even paraphrase Abe Lincoln. You *have* heard of him?"

"You mean the nigger lover…?"

Sarah watched the former corporal snare a creampuff scrap off the platter and slip it into his mouth, thinking that he chewed as he had argued: with toothless precision. She said to him, "Lover or not, Lincoln made the point that books serve to show a man that those original thoughts of his aren't very new after all."

"That's only true if the man writing the book isn't original."

"You miss the point," Sarah said.

"Frau Remley, I speak for a lot of people, who believe what I believe and whether I said it first or not is not the point, as you have pointed out."

"A lot of people…? Herr Hitler, your party has never had anything even close to a slim majority in the Reichstag, but then what matters to you is not the truth, but how you feel, which is fine when you're talking to the masses, but I am one person, something that you forget when you talk to people, one on one—you should work on that."

"There's nothing to work on and so even why belabor the point with someone who doesn't feel the same way?"

"Okay. I'm going to take my clothes off," Sarah said.

"…Right now?"

"Yes, to give you the opportunity to do with your pencil what I should be seeing in art, since I cannot see it in your politics."

"You seem to have no inhibitions."

"Absolutely none," Sarah said. "You should try it."

"I'm not a woman."

"But you are."

"…If you're trying to be clever, you're failing miserably."

"Not at all," Sarah said. "I've seen photos of you in your Nazi uniform and a uniform is like being undressed. It's a man's way of feminizing the male body, without having to admit to having done so."

"It's just the opposite, in fact."

"Herr Hitler, a woman understands clothes on a level that most men don't, and a uniform is nothing but erotica and, like the naked body, it directs your attention to specific parts that are, how shall I say—of interest? But instead of genitalia you wear your medals and party insignia, which proves that your underlying intention is clearly the same."

"Which is…?"

"To seduce, dominate, and control," Sarah said, "and since woman aren't allowed in business and politics, we make best with what's left, and that is why I make it my business to understand people, since they don't bother to do it for themselves—something that I learned from certain a college girl who wrote an interesting paper on the subject that was recently published in a magazine back home."

"Frau Remley, you're not a stupid woman, but your pleasure is to antagonize people and not to help them."

"Herr Hitler, your pleasure is in dismissing them and I dare say eliminating them—but having said that, the real reason that I'm here is to read your fortune."

"…You're kidding me."

"Not at all, Shelby and I happen to be Aryan Norns," Sarah said.

"…. Am I supposed to laugh at that?"

"Unless you're afraid of the truth."

"I'll decide what's true," the former corporal said. "But if you have the power to change the future, then we need to talk."

"Then what you think is power is the opposite of what it really is."

"Go ahead and predict," the former corporal said, expecting Sarah to get up and do something. "…Aren't you going to perform a dance or sing a song first? That's what they usually do."

"We've updated things since then," Sarah said, as she picked up a teaspoon and stared into it. Images came and went out of its hollow bowl that only she could see. She then dropped the spoon to the floor and said, "As I had thought."

"What?"

"The spoon."

"What about it?"

"It landed upside down."

"Which means…?"

"Trouble for you, Herr Hitler."

"What kind of trouble?"

"That kind that will do you in," she said.

"And what kind is that?"

Sarah said, "Your notion of perfection, that which you've written in your book, is a fantasy. As a functioning reality, perfection needs to eliminate anything that gets in its way and that means the truth or anyone else, *including* you, otherwise nothing can be perfect, and you will certainly get in your own way, and that is where your impending doom lies."

"Frau Remley, are you a Jewess?"

"My dear man, are you afraid of me?"

"You scare me little, but there's something about you."

"Something erotic, no doubt," Sarah said, holding onto her smile. "But I'll answer your question, nonetheless. Jesus the Jew once said, 'Whoever wants to be a leader amongst you, must be your servant, and whoever wants to be first amongst you must be the slave of everyone else,' and in that spirit, I *am* a Jew and a proud one at that."

"You'd make a good speaker, if you could only find an audience."

"I'm not looking for one."

"Oh, I forgot," Hitler said, "you're looking for the truth."

"I know the truth when I see it."

"You think you do."

"I *know* I do."

"And *how* do you know you do?"

"Because I measure the truth as I would a man, and it *never* fails."

"And how do you do that?"

"By asking a very simple question," Sarah said.

"And what's that?"

"Would I fuck him—and *you* I wouldn't touch."

The Major entered. His Pistole-Parabellum aimed right at the Austrian's little mustache. "I hope I'm not interrupting anything."

But there was more than one mustache there.

69

Nachzehrer

Death masks atop swaying poles. Skeleton men on stilts. Vulture's beaks and talons. Glockenspiels and jesters. Their caps and bells full of nuisance and hell as the big black head with the little pink hat fell on its side. Ilse pushed through the crowd and kneeled beside Ziggy, her mask removed, the blood from the mortal wound pooling on the street. She said to Ilse, "Go to the castle and say 'Nachzehrer' to the Guardian. Then go to the Crown Prince's chamber, but be quick, as I am quick to die……"

70

I'm Not a Murderer

The flurry of snow atop the castle swirled around the watch towers and whipped through the ramparts, but below the village was quiet. The paraders gone. The narrow streets empty. Only a wayward drunkard or straggler tried to claim the night as chaos had turned into despair. Ilse made her way up the steep narrow path to the castle where just one light burned above. She removed her mask and told the Guardian, "Nachzehrer." He allowed her in. "And where is the Crown Prince's chamber?" The Guardian told her to go through the second door by the mounted stag and continue on through the long hallway and turn into the first passageway and then go to the door with the carving of the prince's crown on it.

Ilse entered the castle proper and trod through the unlit halls. She came upon a choice of turns that the Guardian hadn't bothered to mention. She took the one to the right and continued on, using her hands to find the door, but there were too many. Some small. Some large. Some hadn't been opened for centuries. Unsure of where she was, she turned around and went the other way and, once again, she reached out along the unlit passageway for any door that might be there, but none had the prince's crown on it. She was now angry at the Guardian for not having been clearer, but she well understood that when people explain something they rarely visually sequence what they mean and instead go on and on as if information alone qualifies as directions or instructions. She then felt something on a door and risked striking her last match. In the glow, she could see the filaments of a crown, but then she remembered that the keeper had never said that there was only one door with a crown on it, and what did a prince's crown even look like? She put ear to door. Not a sound was heard. She turned the handle. The door opened. Then, in the available light, she found the Major on the floor, his troubled face bearing the footprint of death.

He quickly brought to mind how we struggle to recruit people to support our make-believe worlds, and when considered real, cities and empires are built, but, when dismissed, desolation and loneliness haunt us as we dream of what could have been.

Two men came in from the antechamber. Ilse narrowed the opening of the door so that they would not see her. They wrapped the Major in a sheet and took him away. She waited then stepped inside. She found a box of matches on the side table and struck one. A man appeared in the glow. She knew him from Egon's dinner parties. He who couldn't keep his eyes off her. Overly polite. Dainty when drinking tea. A man who had no polish, just the wax. Ilse said to the former corporal, "Where is Fräulein Prevette?"

Hitler's eyes, confident in the glow, said, "…What brings you here, Voodoo Child?"

"Where is Fräulein Prevette?"

"You two know each other?"

"Why did you kill the Major?

"No one told me that you knew her."

"What happened here?"

"Mrs. Remley, I'll certainly miss. She does something to a man so that he diverts his anger into another kind of passion."

"Where is Fräulein Prevette?"

"Come with me, Voodoo Child. You look awfully tired. There's coffee and sweets in the next room."

Ilse drew a handgun from her cape and aimed it point blank. "Take another step and I'll kill you."

"Voodoo Child, you'll never get out of here alive if you do. My men are all over. And then you'll never get to see your friends in Paris."

"...Paris?"

"Paris."

"Maybe you killed them as well."

"Don't be stupid. I'm not a murderer," Hitler said.

"You just killed the Major."

"He had a heart attack."

"So will you if you keep it up. Now, why are they going to Paris and not back to Berlin?"

"...Were you and the Major really lovers? Because I heard the gossip but couldn't believe it."

"Why are they going to Paris?"

Hitler said, "Were you sexually active?"

Ilse said, "More lies."

"Well, if you and the Major weren't lovers then why didn't you come with me? I wanted to make you happy."

"...A Jewess making *you* happy?"

"Oh, that," Hitler said. "Just a little lie that we had spread around to drive the Major nuts. You know how politics can be, but my invitation still stands."

"You won't be hearing from me," Ilse said.

"Darling Ilse, you need someone to care for you."

"You're nuts."

"But we talk for hours on end."

"*You* talk for hours on end."

"So does everyone else. ...Did Frau Remley really have sex with that nigger?"

"What brought that up?"

"I merely asked you a question," Hitler said.

"Yeah, but what brought that up?"

"She's perverted."

"But someone peeing on your face isn't?"

"No," Hitler said. "It comes from inside a woman, with all her heat and juices."

"Did she pee on you?"

"No."

"You want me to pee on you?"

"Yes.

"Get on the floor."

He did as he was told, and as she lifted her dress, he thought: The Origin of the World.

When Ilse was done, she backtracked her way out of the castle, looking back every so often into the darkness. She slipped through the portcullis and then down the steep narrow path that led back to town and found Mr. Benchley, the only other person on the street. She removed her mask.

"*Rachel*—I've been looking for all of you. Where's Shelby?"

"Gone."

"What do you mean gone? I've been here forever and haven't seen anyone come out."

"They're all gone," she said, continuing down the path.

"Where?"

"I don't know."

"Why did they let you out and not the rest of them?"

"You're making assumptions again."

"What else am I to do?" Mr. Benchley said, trying to keep up with her. "Where's Mrs. Remley?"

"I don't know."

"Why did they let you out and not Shelby?"

"They tried to kill me, but I got away."

"How did you manage to get away?"

"I'll write a book one day so you can find out."

Mr. Benchley got in front of her and said, "Would any of this have to do with that crazy old woman?"

"What crazy old woman?"

"The one who came up to me at the Fastnacht festival and told me to stay away from you. She said that you're a goddess from some other world."

"Did you believe here?"

"I…I don't know what to believe anymore."

"Then evil has won," Rachel said, as she continued on and disappeared into the night.

Mr. Benchley, undeterred, went up the steep hill to the castle. High above, he saw a single light glowing in the window of the ancient fortress and for a second he had hope, but then the light went out.

www.RaederLomax.com

**Contact the author if you have any questions about the
making of the Midnight Sleeper Series**

http://eepurl.com/b2F_E5

More books by the author

The PREQUEL to the MIDNIGHT SLEEPER SERIES:

STAND YOUR GROUND

How Lawful Mischief Turns Deadly!

KIRKUS Reviews: Stand Your Ground.
"Lomax knows to keep the plot moving…the clipped prose hums
along, generating a blunt, edgy mood."